CAROL ANN DUFFY

Feminine Gospels

PICADOR

In *Feminine Gospels*, Carol Ann Duffy draws on women's experience – both personal and historical – in poems which celebrate, elegize and eroticize the female condition. With themes of beauty, identity and the body, the book tells tall stories as though they were the gospel truth and presents new myths as strange and powerful as the old.

'In the world of British poetry, Carol Ann Duffy is a superstar'
Guardian

Why don't you stop talking

'These are momentous stories of our world as it changes, reflecting and provoking new attitudes and realities. Jackie Kay is a writer of now-times and her stories cry out to be read and absorbed'

Morning Star

'It is the desire for love, which runs through the book like a suppressed howl of anguish, that is the crux of this collection'

Sunday Tribune

'A reader coming for the first time to the work of Jackie Kay might well guess that she's also an accomplished poet. The crispness, tightness and playful sense of humour of the best of her poems is also evident in the baker's dozen of stories that make up this book'

Irish Independent

'This is a book you must put down – and put down frequently – in order to put off reaching the final page'

Evening Herald

'Kay's is a distinctive voice, lucid, occasionally ruthless, sometimes poetic, never self-consciously arty; if stories like these can still be written, the much-maligned short story form must still be alive, not to say kicking'

Irish Times

'There are perfect couplings in *Why Don't You Stop Talking*, where stories of secrets and lies and transformations glance off each other like diamonds spilling out of a pouch and the imagery is twice as dazzling'

Herald

Jackie Kay was born in Edinburgh in 1961 and grew up in Glasgow. She has published three collections of poetry, the first of which, *The Adoption Papers* (Bloodaxe 1991), won the Saltire and Forward Prizes. The second, *Other Lovers* (Bloodaxe 1993), won the Somerset Maugham Award. *Trumpet*, her first novel, won the Author's Club First Novel Award and the *Guardian* Fiction Prize. She lives in Manchester with her son.

Also by Jackie Kay

Trumpet

Jackie Kay

Why don't you stop talking

PICADOR

First published 2002 by Picador

This edition published 2003 by Picador
an imprint of Pan Macmillan Ltd
Pan Macmillan, 20 New Wharf Road, London N1 9RR
Basingstoke and Oxford
Associated companies throughout the world
www.panmacmillan.com

ISBN 0 330 37334 X

Some of these stories have appeared in *Granta*, *You Magazine*, *Damage Land* (Polygon) and *Manchester Short Stories* (Penguin), as well as on Radio 3 and 4.

9 8 7 6 5 4 3

A CIP catalogue record for this book is available from the British Library.

Typeset by Intype London Ltd
Printed and bound in Great Britain by
Mackays of Chatham plc, Chatham, Kent

For Carol Ann

and in memory of

my grandmother,

Margaret Kirk

Contents

Shark! Shark!

He didn't live anywhere near the sea. No haar, no sea mist, no smell of fish, no nets, no boats, no sand. The sea blending into the sky at some distant point in the horizon was a sight he never saw. The relentless, inexhaustible supply of wave after wave after wave, coming again and again and again was something he had done without all of his working life. There he was in the middle of England in the middle of his life. He still couldn't explain why it started to happen, why it kept on happening, why this of all things should have singled him out. It felt personal.

Brian Murphy returned home from work one innocent day, exhausted. He sat himself in the armchair and switched on the TV. Mary was clattering and banging in the kitchen. The teenage sons were up the stairs. The daughter was out. His limbs were heavy. A documentary about sharks was on. The first image Brian saw was the Bull Shark's serrated upper teeth. The unpleasantly excited voice of the nature man was saying that this Bull Shark has a preference for eating baby Sandbar Sharks. He switched the channel, flicking, fast as a fin appearing and disappearing. He couldn't settle on anything. He returned back to the sharks. Stupified, he sat still, sinking into his chair watching the flicking, the flipping, the flashing. He watched in a dwam, in a daze, with dull dark eyes and everything went in, slowly swimming around in his consciousness.

When the sharks had finished, he got up to make himself a piece. Brian Murphy was a Scottish man in the middle of England still fond of his pieces. A piece and jam could calm a man. A cup of strong tea with two sugars. The sound of the kettle. He sat down on his armchair with his piece and his tea and ate, but it was no good and he knew it was no good. He could tell the beginning of something as well as the next man. He could tell because he could feel it right across his chest. Like something lying in wait. Trying to eat that sandwich, it was almost as if his life broke into two pieces: before and after. Brian Murphy couldn't help himself: his own Scottish intuition told him his life was never going to be the same again. He was standing on a big piece of ice and the ice cracked. For Christ's sake, pull yourself together, ya stupid big eedyit, he said to himself. Ya big long drink of water. Why didn't you turn it aff if it wis bothering you?

A week passed and it didn't get better, it got worse. Of course he didn't mention it at the time to his wife or his daughter or his sons. What would they take him for? He was a fitter; he fitted engines to machines. He went to work every day and came back every day and he didn't mention sharks. As best as he could, he tried to fit his life around this terrible business. You would have thought it would be relatively simple living in the middle of England and never ever going to the sea, not even when his wife asked if they could go for a wee day trip as a special anniversary treat. Wrong.

It wasn't just the sea; he refused to go on a ferry, a fishing boat, a canoe. He became wary of his local river, even although he was an intelligent man and it was preposterous. He would be sitting reading the newspaper, flicking through the news when suddenly a sharp shark fact from that bloody documentary would flash into his head for no reason at all. Brian Murphy had seemed to memorize the entire programme by heart as if in his semi-conscious state that pale day, he'd taken every single word into his mind and kept it there. It was locked in his long-term memory now. In 1961, the Bull Shark attacked three people in the mouth of the Limpopo river. He couldn't help himself. The Bull Sharks prefer the murky water, the mouths of rivers. The shallows. Where can you go to be safe if you can be caught out when you're in up to your knees?

Upstream of the Ramu river, on the north-west coast of Papua New Guinea, a shark attacked a teenage girl. She was washing her clothes in the river. The film hadn't shown the girl, it had just shown the river, the spot where it happened. But Brian could picture her well enough, even though he'd never met a girl from Papua New Guinea. Whenever Brian thought about her washing her clothes in the river, he wept. He could see her dark hair, black, flowing down her face and dark skin and bare arms. He pictured a basket empty, waiting for clothes.

And there she was in thigh-deep water. Thigh deep. Not the deep, deep sea. Thigh deep, mind. Witnesses said the shark grabbed the girl around her thigh severing her leg. She died. She died. Blood loss. Brian couldn't help himself; he would try and turn away from such things as all sane people should, turn away and do something ordinary, use his hands. But the moment he turned back round, there was the river with the teenage girl's blood running.

He would be at work, his hands black with engine oil, when, with no prompting at all – face it, what prompting could there be at work in the middle of the country in the middle of the day? – Brian would suddenly become incensed with how long the Great White Shark lives for. Christ, he'd say to himself through gritted teeth, up to one hundred years. Older than I'm going to live. He didn't like to think about that either. His own death moving towards him, under the water, unseen and unsuspected. He would be measuring the space where the new engine was to be fitted when the Great White Shark's likely measurement would rush into his mind, stealing the show. Up to twenty-five-feet long. That's more than four times my height, he thought to himself. He shook his head and stopped for a smoke. He inhaled deep, the smoke swirling around him in front of his face, his fingers stained yellow on the insides.

As he got older, as his teenagers grew up and left home, it didn't get any better. Strange how things intensify when you get older, how your confidence is suddenly shot. Even Brian's speaking voice wasn't as loud as it used to be. A couple of years after his first grandchild appeared, his daughter innocently suggested visiting the aquarium all together, a family thing. Then she said brightly, 'They've got sharks.' 'Out of the question,' Brian said. 'I'm not keen on that sort of thing.' His daughter persisted. Brian exploded. 'I'm not bloody well going, all right. Got it. No way.' Everyone stared at him. He got up and went into the kitchen, belching and burping. He rushed some water into the kettle.

That night Brian got into bed with his wife and huddled up close. He liked to feel her thighs against him in his sleep; her bottom tucked into him. He couldn't get close enough. He nuzzled his chin on her back. 'Give me a bit of space,' Mary said. 'Jesus, I'm near suffocating.' Mary drifted away as if she was floating on water. Brian fell asleep coughing and muttering to himself.

'Brian, Brian, Brian, pet.' Mary shook him awake. He sat bolt upright. 'What's the matter?'

'You were shouting in your sleep. You were shouting strange words in your sleep.'

'What words?' Brian said irritated at being woken up. 'What words?'

'I can't remember properly,' Mary laughed. 'They were strange.'

Brian stared at her bleary-eyed, mystified.

'Oh I remember one now, White Tip, Silver Tip . . . Are they the names of trees, Brian?'

Brian sat bolt upright. 'No, they're the names of sharks?'

'What would you be wanting to shout out the names of sharks for, Brian?'

'How the hell do I know?'

Mary giggled, trying to remember. 'I think one was White Death, is that right?'

'Forget it, Mary. Go back to sleep!'

'Tell me all the names you know now and then you won't say them in your sleep.'

It was worth a try. Mary killed herself laughing as Brian solemnly said, 'Oceanic White Tip, White Pointer, White Death, Van Rooyen's Shark, Slipway Grey Shark . . .'

'Stop! Stop!' Mary howled. 'I'm in fits here.'

'It's not funny!' said Brian.

'Have a laugh at yourself, Brian, it is funny. Where did you get all the names from? Oh God, Oh God,' Mary clutched her sides in the bed. 'I haven't laughed so much in years.' Brian stared bleakly into the night. Mary said, 'Have you been reading up, Brian?'

'No, no. I don't know. I don't know. It was the bloody telly.' Brian could still surprise her after thirty years of marriage. He could wake her up with the names of sharks! Was there was something to be said for a man who could do that? Mary drifted off again, away, gloriously away, oh sleep, oh kind sleep.

Brian was agitated. He shouldn't have said the names out loud; it had made him worse. Now it was his own voice he could hear saying the commentary. He tossed and turned and finally got up and went downstairs. The ironing! Brian would do the ironing to take his mind off things. He was sweating, breathing oddly. He couldn't get this story out of his head. In 1970 a fisherman was working – where was he working? Doesn't matter – in about five foot, *five foot,* of water on his prawn net up a river. That's right it was twelve miles from the sea in Mozambique. A Bull Shark took the fisherman's arm. He stumbled and floundered in the water and, just as he was trying to get his balance, the shark returned and took off his head. There were four of Brian's shirts needing ironing. There were two of Mary's blouses. One pleated skirt. A pleated skirt could take his mind off things. It was hard to get an iron to go down the pleats. Dark, narrow corridors of skirt. Brian got the iron out of the cupboard. He stared at it for a long, panicky moment. Jesus Christ. Even the bloody iron wasn't safe. The iron was a shark's fin, as clear as day. 'You're a stupit man, Brian Murphy,' he said to himself, plugging it in. He put some water in from the tap. He started with Mary's navy pleated skirt. He pulled it over the hard tongue of the board, separating the back of the skirt from the front. The iron hissed and steamed and gulped its own hot breath. Brian thudded the thing back and forth, up and down those pleats, pressing the button that releases the steam frequently. That was a bit better. Thank Christ my old mum taught me to iron, he thought to himself.

Up the stairs he trudged, at four o'clock in the morning, puffing and sorely out of breath, having hung the freshly ironed shirts on the back of chairs in the living room.

He stopped at the top of the stairs to hold his sides and let out a loud breath, like the last breath of a martyr. Mary was snoring, a deep animal sound Brian found quite comforting. He tried to follow the strange strangled rhythms of it, up and down with her chest. Sometimes, inexplicably, the snoring would just cut out, like an engine suddenly stopping. That was frightening. Mary would often wake herself up when she stopped like that and say, 'Oh, Oh Dear,' in a way that would sound as if she were new to herself, as if she was suddenly just being introduced to herself. 'Is that me? Was that me?' she asked. Brian patted her back. Her mouth relaxed again, he could see it in the moonlight that shone through their thin pale curtains. Lips all soft and full of trust. Oh to sleep like Mary. To just fall off and over like that so easy and forget every nagging worry and sleep like Mary slept.

There were the voices too. It wasn't just the horrific pictures. He could hear the many different accents of people around the world, from Mozambique to Miami. Young voices, old, male voices, female. This one was male, from the States. 'I saw a big mouth with big jaws, a great black eye, the dorsal fin and stripes, there were definitely stripes up until its tail.' He tried to push it out of his mind. To visualize his ironing. His striped shirt, oh God, he was back again and so quickly.

At what hour Brian finally drifted off to sleep, he didn't know. He was very bad-tempered the next morning. Couldn't talk for temper. When Mary said, 'Are you all right?' he said, 'Aye Fine, Fine,' like two snaps at her head. He shook his newspaper aggressively. He was all shook up. There was no denying it. This was his last week at work before retirement. Mary wanted to go on a cruise for Christ's sake. They couldn't afford a cruise; Mary always had the big ideas. When he said no, she suggested Miami because their old friends Bill and Jessie were in Miami. He didn't say it. He didn't say it. There was that to be said. But it flashed through his mind. He thought it. He saw the whole ghastly thing again. 1944, Florida. A fisherman caught a large Tiger Shark. Inside he found most of a man's body from the ribs to the knees. The man was never identified. No teeth. 'I don't fancy Miami, Mary,' Brian said. 'Are the Yanks not a bit false?'

'Don't be silly Brian,' Mary said. 'What about going to New Orleans or Mississippi. You've always liked your jazz?'

The Bull Shark has penetrated right down the Mississippi river. Same with the Ganges, same with Sydney Harbour. Rule out Africa. Amanzimtoti, a popular swimming beach in Africa, has a reputation for being the worst shark-attack beach on earth.

How did they leave it for now? With Brian saying he would come up with something. Something away from any water, any sea, any river anywhere. Maybe some place where he and Mary could hide from old age. It was coming. And wasn't it strange? Mary and him starting to stagger about the place, after all that strutting and dancing and waltzing.

Four nights to go before Brian Murphy is no longer a fitter. What will you be fit for? Mary likes to ask him, laughing. Privately she dreads Brian's retirement just when she has got the house to herself, just when she's finally adjusted to not working anymore. The idea of her tall, lanky man with his stooped back, about the house all day in her hair, is stressful. He will not be good at adjusting; Mary knows that about Brian. Hopeless, he'll be hopeless. What will he do with his big hands?

That night Brian wakes sweating again, shouting. Mary sits up and sighs. 'I'll go and sleep in the boys' room,' she says. 'I can't sleep with you at the moment, Brian. You're that restless.' Brian grabs her arm. 'Don't go Mary, please. The Oceanic White Tip is one of the top four most dangerous sharks. It bites for no reason. It might be moving along calmly and suddenly, suddenly, Mary, for no reason, for no reason, Mary, it will just lunge out. Lunge out and attack.' Brian is talking in a terrible whisper as if he has emphysema.

'Stop it, Brian, with all this nonsense, you're frightening me,' Mary says, getting up to go to the boys' room.

'I'm frightened, Mary,' Brian shouts. 'It's me that's bloody terrified.'

'What are you frightened of, Brian,' Mary says, beside herself now with exhaustion and wanting sleep, sleep.

'Sharks,' he says, finally admitting it, a sharp pain going right through his chest at the mention of the word out loud. 'Sharks,' he ventures a second time, this time the word has a jagged, serrated edge carving his heart.

'Oh for goodness sake!' Mary says, 'You're miles away from any shark, Brian.' And she goes off, the back of her white nightie the last nice thing Brian sees, her rounded shoulders, her hair with the rinse running out. She blows him a kiss from the bedroom door. 'I'm going to have to get some sleep, Brian,' she yawns.

Through the wall, Brian can hear Mary snoring. It doesn't reassure him now that he can't see her. It frightens him.

A whole world is going on through there; the beginning of it and the end of it, gasping, choking, throttling. Mary's night-time world as thick as a forest, as secret as trees breathing. Brian breathes in fast shallow sips of air. He can't breathe normally. He's become too aware of his own breath. He could gag on it. If only he could forget it, forget the gnawing, gnashing anxiety and breathe normally. His chest is tight as if the whole apparatus had been locked inside, something like treasure from a sunken ship. He coughs and coughs to try to normalize his breathing, shock himself out of it. But the panic is still there, tight, rapier sharp. He claws off his pyjama shirt. Too hot. Christ, far too hot. He gets up and opens his bedroom window. Too stuffy. No air. Too bloody muggy.

Outside in his street there are no seagulls whirring. There is no noise of the sea thrashing against rocks, waves rolling over shingle. No sea cliff for lemmings. No combers, no breakers, no surf, no spume. No choppiness. No white horses. Brian Murphy lives nowhere near the sea. No cataclysmic tidal waves. There is not even the gargle of a river rinsing its own mouth. Brian feels his own saliva bubble in his mouth and dribble down his chin. A slow, sleepy rain, all patter and smirr, dreams in his street. Most of the neighbours' lights are off except for Jeanette Cochrane next door who is an insomniac, and the new people four houses down. Brian feels an empathy with Jeanette in the dark. If she were to look out her window now, everything might be all right. But she doesn't. The street is period-dark with the strange unhealthy glow of the yellow street lamps. The sky is a mass of stars and clouds. Brian runs his hands through his hair. Never did go bald did Brian. Kept his own hair. He coughs again.

Brian Murphy's grandmother told him that when she was ten in 1852, she had whooping cough. She came from Sutherland in the north of Scotland. A live trout was put into her mouth, head first so that she could feel the trout breathe inside her mouth. It was supposed to cure her of the whooping cough, the fish's breath. It was a story that haunted Brian as a boy, so much so he wished he'd never been told it. Now, here it came again for no reason in the middle of the night. His child-grandmother standing in her kitchen with a trout in her mouth.

Human beings who have survived the unthinkable have said that the shark, whilst attacking them, *looked right through them.* It is this, more than anything else that chills Brian's blood till his blood is darker than dark red. The notion of a shark staring you right in the face. By then there would be nowhere else to go, no hiding place, just a terrible nauseating certainty facing you, inevitable like death.

He goes down the stairs and into his living room. He switches on the light. There's something odd about disturbing your own living room in the middle of the night; the sofa and the armchairs look as if they were not expecting you, you who could now so easily be a total stranger, an intruder, an impostor. Brian sits down on his own chair but it doesn't feel as familiar as it did during the daytime. It feels wrong. He should have stayed up there with his fears rather than have brought them down here. He picks up the paper, the news seems days old. He can hardly believe it was just this morning that he was reading about the pathologist who misdiagnosed hundreds of cases. Is Brian a case? he wonders, Am I a case? A basket case. How can people be cases? Brian's got a leathery face. He flips over quickly. He doesn't like health stories, health scares. The whole country's gone health-mad.

The pressure behind Brian Murphy's breastbone seems to be on the move, shooting more pain up into his throat and down his left arm. He sees his grandmother again, at ten, with a trout in her mouth. She is in sepia and so is the trout. The trout suits sepia; it flatters the fish. How can grandmothers be wee girls, how could they ever have been wee girls? Brian had asked himself this when he was a boy hearing the story and now he is a grandfather himself. All in the blink of an eye; all in the flip of a trout. Nobody believes it till it happens to him or her. Mary and him have been married now thirty-four years. Mary knows Brian better than anybody in the world and Brian knows Mary better than anybody in the world; or they should do by now. Yet Mary can't soothe Brian about sharks and Brian can't admit the extent of his fears.

What's bugging him now is this holiday. First it was the cruise, then Miami, now Mary's got it into her head that she wants to go to Australia for three months to visit her brother. Australia for Christ's sake! Every weird shark that ever showed its ugly mug has been sighted in Australia. The Megamouth Shark, extremely rare, yet spied in Australia. Small eyes and a huge bulbous mouth, sinister and gangsterish. It swims in stiff slow movements; similar probably to the way Brian swims these days if he manages to force himself down to the local pool. Brian gets up and puts the kettle on. If only Mary would hear him up in the night and come down and join him. But Mary is in deep with her sleep, no chance. Maybe something warm will loosen the constriction. He puts on the kitchen light. Everything is clean and tidy, scrubbed. Everything has been put away for the next day on the understanding that there will be a next day. Brian is sweating. It is unusual for Brian to sweat. He is not a sweaty man. Nobody has ever had a whiff of his oxters and held their noses behind his back. But he is sweating now and he can smell something. A smell that doesn't seem his, sour and frightening.

He stirs two sugars into his tea and gets the milk out of the fridge. The light comes on in the fridge, quite a wee comfort to a man up in the middle of the night. He puts the milk bottle back, closes the door gently. Outside, the darkness is beginning to peel away slowly, slowly till it will eventually arrive at its heart of light. The birds will open soon, like a play in the West End. And when they start their cacophony Brian Murphy will know another day is going to go on and that he is safe from the shark. The Goblin Shark's body is slender and flabby. It hunts prey by sensing their electrical fields. There have been reports that its teeth have been found embedded in underwater electrical cables.

He sits down in his armchair. Does he feel a bit better? He tells himself he feels a bit better, but he can't be sure. He tries to force himself to feel better to say, 'C'mon, Brian son, c'mon, rally yirsell,' but the tight bar across his chest is still bearing down. Why does he not just tell Mary about the sharks: how all his life he would have liked to have pretended they didn't exist; how just the mention of one of their names – Megamouth Shark, Hammerhead Shark, Thresher Shark, Basking Shark – sends Brian demented. Pictures swim in front of his eyes. Whitish spots that cover the dark body of the whale shark. Three hundred rows of very tiny teeth.

If he was out at sea, if he was out at sea swimming in good faith off the coast of one place or another, Africa, Australia, America, if he was out at sea and a shark saw him, that shark would decide whether to pick him up now or later. What does his life mean to a shark? Would the shark know he had been an engineer, a father, a fitter, a grandfather, a son, a grandson, a boy, a man, an old man? Would the shark care? Brian takes a sup of his tea. The shark wouldn't care. Brian gets up and shuts the living room door. He closes the door that leads to the kitchen. He should call the doctor but he hates doctors as much as he hates sharks. Some doctors are sharks.

White coats – opportunists doing private and NHS. He should call the doctor and tell him he has a pain in his chest that will not go away. He should shout for Mary. He doesn't have the energy to climb the stairs. He is out of breath already. He goes back into the kitchen, makes another cup of tea, hanging on to the Formica surface. He sits back down in his living room.

If he did manage up the stairs to shake Mary awake, to shout, *Mary Wake up I'm going to die*, Mary would tell him not to be so silly. And she'd be right. Death is silly. It makes your whole life silly. Brian's slippers are silly. His dominoes, his sports page, his love of his sons, his trade unionism, his fringe, his temper, his love of cream crackers, Perry Como, Banks Bitter. All silly. All ridiculous. To bother getting attached when it's meaningless. All of his life he told himself this would never happen to him.

He tells himself that now. A bit of peace and quiet. Try and drink the hot tea. Try and drink. Hot tea. He can see himself as a scrawny wee boy with reddish cheeks and fair hair flowing over his face. When did his hair grow dark? Bare knees. Thank God no one ever put a live trout in his mouth. He would have died there and then at ten if that trout had gone in his mouth. You couldn't live on under such circumstances, having been compromised in such a way with a fucking fish in your mouth for Christ sake.

He drifts off. His mouth wide open, filtering the air. He gasps for breath. He feels as if he is being strangled. Not all sharks are dangerous. A Japanese snorkeller did once manage to get sucked into a Whale Shark's mouth but was quickly spat out again. Imagine being spat out of a shark's mouth. Maybe that will happen to him when the moment comes. He'll be sent right back to try again. That will be what it's like for some people, thumped on the chest and sent back to try again.

Suddenly Brian Murphy throws back his head and bellows out a roar with no language, no accent. A roar that he himself hears, away, away in the distance across the sea. It seems to rise up out of his throat from deep, deep down in his heart. His face swells and turns purple. His eyes bulge forward. He feels himself reach out for something before he collapses. The light outside comes up slowly, gradually. He feels the light within him lift its frail skirt. He takes one massive long gurgling watery breath, and dies. On the other side, the sharks eat the corpses that float on the Ganges.

Inside Brian Murphy's fibrous sack, the heart is still wriggling, twitching. His lungs need oxygen; his heart needs blood. Brian Murphy's pupils are wide and black, dilated so much that it would seem his brain has died.

In the morning, the proper morning, not the dead morning, not the insomniac birdsong morning, but the ordinary morning, long after the milkman has been and the paper delivered and the post has come, Mary comes down the stairs, yawning and saying, 'Oh dear, I'm still tired' to herself, pleasantly. There is so much innocence in that little yawn-sigh sound coming downstairs that Brian, if he could, would give anything not to shatter it, not to blast and obliterate it, with his own dead body lying there to greet her. He would give anything for it all not to be true, for sharks to have never existed, for nobody ever to have got hurt.

Big milk

The baby wasn't really a baby anymore except in the mind of the mother, my lover. She was two years old this wet summer and already she could talk buckets. She even had language for milk. Big Milk and Tiny Milk. One day I saw her pat my lover's breasts in a slightly patronizing fashion and say, 'Silly, gentle milk.' Another day we passed a goat with big bells round its neck in a small village near the Fens. The light was strange, mysterious. The goat looked like a dream in the dark light. The baby said, 'Look, Big Milk, Look, there's a goat!' The baby only ever asked Big Milk to look at things. Tiny Milk never got a look in.

I never noticed that my lover's breasts were lop-sided until the baby started naming them separately. The baby was no mug. The left breast was enormous. The right one small and slightly cowed in the presence of a great twin. Big Milk. I keep saying the words to myself. What I'd give for Big Milk now. One long suck. I was never that bothered about breasts before she had the baby. I wasn't interested in my own breasts or my lover's. I'd have the odd fondle, but that was it. Now, I could devour them. I could spend hours and hours worshipping and sucking and pinching. But I'm not allowed. My lover tells me her breasts are milk machines only for the baby. 'No,' she says firmly, 'They are out of bounds.' My lover says I should understand. 'You are worse than a man,' she tells me. A man would understand, she says. A man would defer. I'm not convinced. A man would be more jealous than I am. Two years. Two years is a long time to go without a single stroke. I look over her shoulder at the baby pulling the long red nipple of Big Milk back and forth.

At night I lie in bed next to the pair of them sleeping like family. The mother's arms flung out like a drowned bird. The baby suckling like a tiny pig. The baby isn't even aware that she drinks warm milk all night long. She is in the blissful world of oblivion. Limbs all soft and gone. Full of my own raging insomnia, I test the baby's hand. The small fat hand lands back down on the duvet with a plump. She doesn't even stir. I try my lover's hand. She can tell things in her sleep. She knows the difference between the baby and me. In her sleep, she pulls away, irritated. I lie next to the sleeping mother and baby and feel totally irreligious. They are a painting. I could rip the canvas. I get up and open the curtains slightly. Nobody stirs. I take a peek at the moon. It looks big and vain, as if it's saying there is only one of me, buster, there's plenty of you suckers out there staring at me. It is a canny moon tonight, secretive. I piss the loudest piss I can manage. I pour a glass of water. Then I return to bed next to the sleeping mother and daughter. The baby is still suckling away ferociously, her small lips going like the hammers. It is beyond belief. How many pints is that she's downed in the one night. No wonder the lover is drained. The baby is taking everything. Nutrients. Vitamins. The lot. She buys herself bottles and bottles of vitamins but she doesn't realize that it is pointless; the baby has got her. The baby has moved in to occupy her, awake or asleep, night or day. My lover is a saint, pale, exhausted. She is drained dry. The hair is dry. Her hair used to gleam.

I'm not bothered about her hair. I am not bothered about not going out anymore, anywhere. The pictures, pubs, restaurants, the houses of friends. I don't care that I don't have friends anymore. Friends without babies are carrying on their ridiculous, meaningless lives, pretending their silly meetings, their silly movies, their uptight nouvelle cuisine meals matter. Getting a haircut at Toni and Guy to cheer themselves up. Or spending a whole sad summer slimming. Or living for the two therapy hours per week. Getting up at six to see a shrink at seven. That's what they are up to. A few of them still bang away at ideas that matter to them. But even they sound tired when they talk about politics. And they always say something shocking to surprise me, or themselves. I don't know which. I don't see any of them anymore.

What do I see? I see the baby mostly. I see her more than I see my lover. I stare into her small face and see her astonishing beauty the way my lover sees it. The big eyes that are a strange green colour. The lavish eyelashes. The tiny perfect nose. The cartoon eyebrows. The perfect baby-soft skin. The lush little lips. She's a picture. No doubt about it. My lover used to tell me that I had beautiful eyes. I'd vainly picture my own eyes when she paid me such compliments. I'd see the deep rich chocolate-brown melt before me. The long black lashes. But my eyes are not the subject these days. Or the object, come to think of it. My eyes are just for myself. I watch mother and daughter sleeping peaceably in the dark. Dreaming of each other, probably. There are many nights I spend like this, watching. I haven't made up my mind yet what to do with all my watching. I am sure it will come to some use. The baby dribbles and the lover dribbles. The light outside has begun. I've come round again. The birds are at it. The baby has the power. It is the plain stark truth of the matter. I can see it as I watch the two of them. Tiny puffs of power blow out of the baby's mouth.

She transforms the adults around her to suit herself. Many of the adults I know are now becoming babified. They talk a baby language to each other. They like the same food. They watch *Teletubbies*. They read Harry Potter. They even go to bed at the same time as the baby; and if they have a good relationship they might manage whispering in the dark. Very little fucking. Very little. I'm trying to console myself here. It's another day.

In the morning the baby always says hello to me before my lover gets a word in. To be fair, the baby has the nicest hello in the whole world. She says it like she is showering you with bluebells. You actually feel cared for when the baby talks to you. I can see the seduction. I know why my lover is seduced. That and having her very own likeness staring back at her with those strange green eyes. I can never imagine having such a likeness. I tell myself it must be quite creepy going about the place with a tiny double. A wee doppelgänger. It's bound to unsettle you a bit, when you are washing your hair, to look into the mirror and for one moment see a tiny toddler staring back at you. It can't be pleasant.

The feeding itself isn't pleasant either. Not when the baby has teeth. I've heard my lover howl in agony on more than one occasion when the baby has sunk her sharp little milk teeth into Big Milk. A woman is not free till her breasts are her own again. Of this I am certain. I am more certain of this than a woman's right to vote or to choose. As long as her breasts are tied to her wean she might as well be in chains. She can't get out. Not for long. She rushes home with her breasts heavy and hurting. Once we went out for a two-hour-and-twenty-minute anniversary meal. When we got home my lover teemed up the stairs and hung over the bathroom sink. The milk spilled and spilled. She could have shot me with it there was so much. Big gun milk. It was shocking. She swung round and caught me staring, appalled. She looked proud of the quantities. Said she could have filled a lot of bottles, fed a lot of hungry babies with that.

I tried to imagine the state of my life with my lover feeding hundreds of tiny babies. I pictured it for a ghastly moment: our new super king-size bed invaded by babies from all over the world. My lover lying in her white cotton nightie. The buttons open.

Big Milk and Tiny Milk both being utilized for a change. Tiny Milk in her element – so full of self-importance that for a second Tiny Milk has bloated into the next cup size. The next time she mentioned having enough milk to feed an army, I told her she had quite enough on her hands. And she laughed sympathetically and said my name quite lovingly. I was appeased for a moment until the baby piped up with a new word. 'Did you hear that?' she said, breathless. 'That's the first time she's ever said that. Isn't that amazing?'

'It is,' I said, disgusted at myself, her and the baby all in one fell swoop. 'It's totally amazing – especially for her age,' I added slyly. 'For her age, it is pure genius.'

She plucked the baby up and landed a smacker on her smug baby cheek. The baby patted Big Milk again and said, 'Funny, funny, Milk. Oh look, Mummy, Milk shy.' The baby's fat little hand was trying to pull the breast out again. I left the two of them to it on the landing outside the toilet.

Even when I go up to my attic I can still hear them down below. Giggling and laughing, singing and dancing together. 'If you go down to the woods today, you're in for a big surprise.' The rain chaps on my tiny attic windows. Big Milk is having a ball. I climb down the steep stairs to watch some more. Daytime watching is different from night-time. Tiny details light up. The baby's small hands are placed protectively on the soft full breasts. The mouth around the nipple. Sometimes she doesn't drink. She just lies half asleep, contemplating milk or dreaming milk. It makes me wonder how I survived. I was never breastfed, myself. My mother spoon-fed me for two weeks then left. I never saw her again. Perhaps I've been dreaming of her breasts all my life. Maybe that's what rankles with the baby taking Big Milk for granted. When her mouth expectantly opens there is no question that the nipple won't go in. No question. Every soft, open request is answered. I try and imagine myself as a tiny baby, soft black curls on my head, big brown eyes. Skin a different colour from my mother's. I imagine myself lying across my mother's white breast, my small brown face suffocating in the pure joy of warm, sweet milk. The smell of it, recognizing the tender smell of it. I imagine my life if she had kept me. I would have been a hairdresser if I hadn't been adopted. I'm quite sure. I would have washed the dandruff off many an old woman's head. I would have administered perms to give them the illusion of their hair forty years before. I would have specialized in tints and dyes, in conditioners that give full body to the hair. I would probably have never thought about milk. The lack of it. Or the need of it.

I lie in the dark with the rain playing soft jazz on the windowpane of our bedroom. I say our bedroom, but it is not our bedroom any more. Now teddy bears and nappies and ointment and wooden toys and baby clothes can be found strewn all over the floor. I lie in the dark and remember what it was like when I had my lover all to myself. When she slept in my arms and not the baby's. When she woke up in the night to pull me closer. When she muttered things into my sleeping back. I lie awake and remember all the different places my lover and I had sex. All the different ways, when we had our own private language. The baby has monopolized language. Nothing I say can ever sound so interesting, so original. The baby has converted me into a bland, boring, possessive lover who doesn't know her arse from her elbow. There are bits of my body that I can only remember in the dark. They are not touched. The dawn is stark and obvious. I make my decision. I can't help it. It is the only possible thing I can do under the circumstances.

Don't doubt I love my lover and I love her baby. I love their likeness. Their cheeks and eyes. The way their hair moves from their crown to scatter over their whole head in exactly the same place. Their identical ears. I love both of them. I love the baby because she is kind. She would never hurt anybody. She is gentle, silly. But love is not enough for me this time. I get up, get dressed and go outside with my car keys in my hand. I close my front door quietly behind me. My breath in my mouth. I take the M61 towards Preston. I drive past four junction numbers in the bleached morning. There are few cars on the road. I stop at a service station and drink a black coffee with two sugars. I smoke two cigarettes that taste disgusting because it is too early. I don't smoke in the day usually. I smoke at night. Day and night have rolled into one. The baby's seat in the back is empty. The passenger seat has a map on it. There is no lover to read the map, to tell me where to go. There is no lover to pass me an apple. There is just me and the car and the big sky, flushed with the morning. I put on a tape and play some music. I am far north now. Going further. I am nearly at the Scottish border. I feel a strange exhilaration. I know my lover and her baby are still sleeping, totally unaware of my absence. As I drive on past the wet fields of morning, I feel certain that there is not a single person in the world who truly cares about me. Except perhaps my mother. I have finally found out where she lives up north. Right at the top of the country in a tiny village, in a rose cottage. She lives in the kind of village where people still notice a stranger's car. If I arrive in the middle of the day, the villagers will all come out and stare at my car and me. They will walk right round my car in an admiring circle. Someone might offer to park it for me.

I will arrive in daytime. When I knock at the door of Rose Cottage, my mother will answer. She will know instantly, from the colour of my skin, that I am her lost daughter. Her abandoned daughter. I have no idea what she will say. It doesn't matter. It doesn't matter if she slams the door in my face, just as long as I can get one long look at her breasts. Just as long as I can imagine what my life would have been like if I had sucked on those breasts for two solid years. If she slams the door and tells me she doesn't want to know me, it will pierce me, it will hurt. But I will not create a scene in a Highland town. I will go to the village shop and buy something to eat. Then I will ask where the nearest hair salon is. I will drive there directly where a sign on the window will read, ASSISTANT WANTED. I will take up my old life as a hairdresser. When I say my old life, I mean the life I could have, perhaps even should have, led. When I take up my old life, old words will come out of my mouth. Words that local people will understand. Some of them might ask me how I came to know them. When they do, I will be ready with my answer. I will say I learned them with my mother's milk.

I am off the M6 now and on the A74. I read somewhere that the A74 is the most dangerous road in the country. Something new in me this morning welcomes the danger. Something in me wants to die before I meet my mother. When I think about it, I realize that I have always wanted to die. That all my life, I have dreamed longingly of death. Perhaps it was because she left. Perhaps losing a mother abruptly like that is too much for an unsuspecting baby to bear. I know now this minute, zooming up the A74 at 110 miles per hour, that I have wanted to die from the second she left me. I wonder what she did with the milk in her breasts, how long it took before it dried up, whether or not she had to wear breast pads to hide the leaking milk. I wonder if her secret has burned inside her Catholic heart for years.

I can only give her the one chance. Only the one. I will knock and I will ask her to let me in. But if she doesn't want me, I won't give her another chance. I won't give anyone another chance. It has been one long dance with death. I have my headlights on even though there is plenty of daylight. I have them on full beam to warn other cars that I am a fast bastard and they had better get out of my way. I play my music softly. The blue light on my dashboard is lit up. Is there anyone out there behind or before me on the A74 who has ever felt like this? I realize that I am possibly quite mad. I realizc that the baby has done it to me. It is not the baby's fault or her mother's. They can't help being ordinary. Being flesh and blood. The world is full of people who are separated from their families. They could all be on the A74 right now, speeding forwards to trace the old bloodline. It is like a song line. What would have been my mother's favourite song? 'Ae Fond Kiss'? 'Ae fond kiss and then we sever.' There is much to discover. I picture the faces of all the other manic adopted people, their anonymous hands clutched to the steering wheel in search of themselves. Their eyes are all intense. I have never met an adopted person who does not have intense eyes. But they offer no comfort. This is all mine.

Exhausted, I arrive in the village at three o'clock. My mouth is dry, furry. It is a very long time since I have slept. I spot a vacancy sign outside a place called the Tayvallich Inn. It has four rooms, three taken. The woman shows me the room and I tell her I'll take it. It is not a particularly pleasant room, but that doesn't matter. There is no view. All I can see from the window is other parts of the inn. I close the curtains. The room has little light anyway. I decide to go and visit my mother tomorrow after sleep. When I get into the small room with the hard bed and the nylon sheets, I weep for the unfairness of it all. A picture of the baby at home, in our Egyptian cotton sheets suckling away and smiling in her sleep flashes before me. My lover's open nightie. It occurs to me that I haven't actually minded all my life. My mother shipping me out never bothered me. I was happy with the mother who raised me, who fed me milk from the dairy and Scot's porridge oats and plumped my pillows at night. I was never bothered at all until the baby arrived. Until the baby came I never gave any of it a moment's thought. I realize now in room four of Tayvallich Inn under the pink nylon sheets that the baby has engineered this whole trip. The baby wanted me to go away. She wanted her mother all to herself in our big bed. Of late, she's even started saying, 'Go away!' It is perfectly obvious to me now. The one thing the baby doesn't lack is cunning. I turn the light on and stare at the silly brown and cream kettle, the tiny wicker basket containing two sachets of Nescafé, two tea bags, two bags of sugar and two plastic thimbles of milk. I open one thimble and then another with my thumbnail. They are the size of large nipples. I suck the milk out of the plastic thimbles. The false milk coats my tongue. I am not satisfied. Not at all. I crouch down to look into the mirror above the dressing table. I am very pale, very peely-wally. Big dark circles under my eyes. I do not look my best for my mother. But why should that matter? A mother should love her child unconditionally. My hair needs combing. But I have brought nothing with me. I did not pack a change of clothes. None of it matters.

I pass the nosy inn woman in the hall. She asks me if I need anything. I say, 'Yes, actually, I need a mother.' The woman laughs nervously, unpleasantly, and asks me if I'll be having the full Scottish breakfast in the morning. I tell her I'm just not sure what will be happening. She hesitates for a moment and I hesitate too. Before she scurries off to tell her husband, I notice her eyes are the colour of strong tea. I open the door that now says NO VACANCIES and head for Rose Cottage. I can't wait for tomorrow, I must go today. I must find her today. My heart is in my mouth. I could do it with my eyes shut. I feel my feet instinctively head in the right direction. It is teatime. My mother will be having her tea. Perhaps she will be watching the news. My feet barely touch the ground. The air is tart and fresh in my face. Perhaps some of my colour will return to my cheeks before my mother opens her front door. Will she tilt her head to the side gently when she looks at me? Following my nose miraculously works. There in front of me is a small stone cottage. Outside the roses are in bloom. There is a wonderful yellow tea-rose bush. I bend to sniff one of the flowers. I feel the impossible softness of the rose petals crush against my nose. I sink towards the sweet, trusting scent. I always knew she would like yellow roses. I stare at the front door. It is painted plain white. Standing quietly next to the front door are two bottles of milk. I open the silver lid of one of them and drink, knocking it back on the doorstep. It is sour. It is lumpy. I test the other one. It is sour as well. A trickle of thin sour milk pours through the thick stuff. I look into my mother's house through the letterbox. It is dark in there. I can't see a single thing.

Why don't you stop talking

I saw her looking at me filling my trolley with chocolate biscuits. I weren't imagining things because she had one of them stuck-up looks on her face and I weren't having it. I've got too old to take any more crap. I know myself and I know other people. And I know when someone's coming over all judgemental. And she was. So I said to her, 'Life's too short to worry about having a fat arse.' She said, 'Sorry?' I said, 'You were looking in my trolley.' She looked around herself the way that people do when they've decided they are with a fruitcase, a total nutter. She walked off pushing her trolley down the aisle towards the bumper bags of crisps. But I weren't having it. You take enough, and one day you don't take no more. So I followed her with my trolley, nudged her in the elbow and I said to her, 'Watch your weight do you?' and she turned and said, 'Look, I wasn't looking at your biscuits for the reasons you think.' She were very well-spoken. I were shocked because she admitted she *was* looking into my trolley. I hadn't been imagining things. I knew I hadn't. She pushed her trolley away from me, but you can't leave me with a cliff-hanger like that. I followed her and said, 'What reasons then?' And she said, 'None of your business,' and walked off again rounding the corner to the long fridges. I saw her put some cottage cheese in her trolley and a tub of something.

I could tell she was a shy one. The shy don't talk enough. She was needing someone like me to coax her out of herself. I made sure I finished my shopping when she did and stood behind her in the checkout queue. It takes a lot for me to say sorry to anybody because nine times out of ten I am right. This time I decided I wanted to hear more and I said to her, 'Sorry about that earlier. It's the old paranoia.' She was loading her stuff on to the belt and her stuff was all very healthy. Tubs of cottage cheese. Bags of lettuce, spring onions, those tomatoes still on their vines, red apples, a small wrinkled melon and something weird I don't know the name of, but next time I come I might look for one and have it.

She flushed red in the face. She were quite a looker. The checkout girl was eyeing me suspiciously and looking uncomfortable. The shy one didn't reply. I waited but she didn't say nothing. I said to her, 'You don't look like a stuck-up cow, are you a stuck-up cow?' It were too late. It had just popped out my mouth and nothing stopping it. It's harder to take words back than it is to get a refund. The checkout girl looked at me frightened like as if I was carrying a gun. I could see that she were contemplating doing something like calling the supermarket manager. The shy one looked straight at me, coolly and said, 'Why don't you stop talking?'

I have to admit she had a point there. I do have one of those tongues that gets me into a load of trouble. I can't help myself. I just come out with what's in my head and it has caused me terrible problems all my life. I don't know if it's just that it was the tongue I was born with and I couldn't do nothing about it or what. Sometimes it even feels like the words are not my decisions, like somebody else is talking with my tongue. Other times it feels like a big affliction like a harelip or a cleft palate. I'd rather have a lisp, or a stutter. I wouldn't mind one of them bad stammers, then so much damage wouldn't be done cos the stammer would slow me down. She weren't the first one that has said that to me. I held up my hand and said, 'Fair enough, you want me to stop talking, but all I wanted to know was why you were looking in my trolley?'

She turned round quite vicious like, her beautiful looks all changed, her mouth snarling and she said to me, 'You're one of those people that just doesn't know when to stop. Get yourself a shrink.' I hadn't figured her for the nasty type somehow so that quite shocked me. I'd thought she was nice. I didn't usually get people so wrong. My big breasts felt suddenly bigger and I crossed my arms in front of myself. Actually I wanted to ram my trolley into the backs of her rayon nylon tights, but I can exercise control when I want to. I'm never violent with my fists. She packed her healthy stuff. She had some order to the way she was doing it. And then she left. I had to load my ten packets of chocolate HobNobs, my three packs of Jaffas, my Penguins, my KitKats and my two packs of mini chocolate rolls on to the conveyor belt and give the girl a look that said, 'What are you looking at?' so as she would keep it belted. I didn't say nothing to her but I was dying to tell her how that stuck-up cow was in the wrong and I was in the right. The times I am silent when I need to talk is as hard as bursting for a piss. I can feel the talk coming and it's like a physical thing. I rushed outside and talked to myself behind the recycling bins where nobody could see me except an old alkie who was rummaging through some discarded bottles which hadn't made it inside either the brown or the green or the white bins. He was swallowing the dregs of wine and rainwater from green bottles and he hardly paid me any attention at all. His trousers were wet at the front.

All the way home that sentence of hers was right in my head and I said it to myself out loud. When I were four I was staying at my nan's for a few days while my mum was in hospital. I was talking away to my nan about the little friend I'd found one day in the square of green outside her high-rise flat in Hackney. The little girl was wearing bright red trousers and red wellie boots. I told my nan how I'd gone again down to the square of green and she'd disappeared and she was funny because she'd been telling me her sister was a 'whiny little swine' and I'd never heard somebody as little as me say 'swine.' Suddenly my nan said to me, 'Thelma, stop the yabbering and the blabbering, you're tiring me out you are,' and I was shocked, but I kept on telling her all about the girl. How she was smaller in height than me and how she had carrot colour hair and where did my nan think she had gone. I'd been looking for her every day now for ages. How could my nan find her? My nan said, 'Right, that does it, I'll have to fetch the Red Loony Van Men. The Red Loony Van Men will come for you and take you to the asylum, to the mental home where you'll learn to hold that tongue of yours.' And to my total horror, she got up and put on her mackintosh, doing up the buttons as fast as she could manage, and put her triangle of patterned scarf over her head, tying it tightly, no-nonsense like, under her chin and left the house. I watched her from the window, small and definite below me. I were in a right state. I imagined the inside of the Red Loony Van: there would be cruel-eyed men with ropes to tie me up and Alsatians to keep guard. I can remember it exactly as if I'd actually been bundled into the back of it. My nan were strict but I still loved her like nothing else. I slept with her when I were there in her big high bed. I cried looking down at her as I watched her disappear up the street. She came back half an hour later with a fish supper but by that time the Red Loony Van Men were taking up the whole of my head and I couldn't eat and I were silent for some time. She might have regretted what she'd done cos she kept saying, 'What's the matter with you, cat got your tongue?'

All my family used to talk a lot except my nan and my silent brother. He hardly spoke but then that was because he had nothing in his head. My mother talked a lot. You couldn't get a word in with her.

And she could be vicious with her tongue. I'd rather she'd hit me than have heard the half of what she said to me. My dad talked with his hands and his mouth when he was around. My dad was from Jamaica and my mum were a real East Ender. I don't see them anymore and they don't see each other. One Christmas we all said things we shouldn't and once they were said we couldn't get over them. I reckon families should be banned. They should find some other way of doing it.

I was feeling rattled and when I'm feeling rattled the thoughts speed up inside my head and I can't get any peace. I walked slowly towards the Tube because I can't walk fast because I'm carrying a fat arse. I laughed to myself, swinging it down the High Street. The litter was blowing this way and that and the place was filthy. Somebody ought to clear this street up. It's a disgrace. I stopped to get some money out with my card from the wall.

I were just getting my card out when this big geezer pushed in, jumping the queue. I said to him. 'I was here first.' He said, 'You were mucking about with your handbag, I'm in a hurry.' I could tell the geezer looked the dangerous type because he had a bad face, but that didn't stop me. If I feel wronged, I have to speak up. Simple as that. You can't go about life letting people get away with things.

I said, 'You know what's wrong with you, don't you? You got no manners. Have you always been like that pushing in front of women? Did your mother not teach you no manners? I'm talking to you.' He was checking his balance. I was standing quite close to him. I could see he had a lot more money than me. 'You think cos you're rich you can jump queues?' I said to him. He turned round taking his notes and putting them in his wallet. He had broad shoulders. 'You're lucky I have got manners,' he said to me. 'If I didn't I'd belt you one on that fat black mouth of yours!' He got into his black car which he'd parked half on the pavement, half on double yellow lines. I shouted at his car, 'I'll report you, asshole!' I were shaking again.

Get yourself home, Thelma. Get yourself home. Some days are just sent to try you. As soon as you get up you know it's going be giving it to you all day. I was trying to walk quickly and puffing and sweating. All of a sudden, I didn't feel safe. The sun was shining for a change but it wasn't making me happy. People can't really cope with the heat in this country. They bake and they sweat and they wear the wrong things. I noticed an ice cream cone lying on the street melting.

It was her voice I heard first. It were so loud and shrill. I told myself to walk on but I couldn't help but notice that she was shaking her child, back and forth, on the street, really shaking him like he were a rag doll. She was a young woman. I can't stand nobody being unkind to kids, so I said to her, 'Easy does it, love, he's just a little fellow.' I was trying to be careful and not antagonize the woman. She stared at me with her mouth full open as if she hadn't heard right, then she said, 'Mind your own fucking business. He's not just a little fellow, he's a fucking psychopath, he's been winding me up all day and he fucking knows it. Don't you?' she said, turning her attentions to the little guy again and jabbing him while he screamed red in the face. I never heard of anyone accusing a two year old of being a psycho.

I said to her, 'You must just be stressed out. Don't take it out on him. What can he do?' She thought I'd gone cos she whirled back around to me, turning her head away from the screaming toddler who was now giving it big licks. 'Beat it!' she shouted at me. 'Shut your fucking trap!'

It was something I'd been noticing more and more on the London streets. How many mothers swear these days, really bad swearing. Not just bloody and damn. But Cs and Fs and stuff. I said to her, 'You ought to wash out your mouth, swearing like that in front of your kid!' Out it came, I couldn't help myself. I saw her coming. She came right up to me, still holding the toddler in one arm. She slapped my face really hard so that it stung. The toddler stopped crying all of a sudden. She said, 'I told you to shut it. Who do you think you are you fat interfering cow?' She was skinny and wiry and had sharp features like a fox. She was pushing me with one hand as she spoke, rhythmic like. She was strong too. Strong arms, must train at the gym. I was scared she was going to knock me right down. I said, 'I was only trying to help.' She stopped pushing. 'Help? Don't kid yourself. You don't know what I've been through this morning. Piss off before I kick the shit out of your fat arse.' I walked off, quite shaken up I was, my arse swinging, indignant. When I'd got a few hundred yards away from her I shouted, 'You need help. You should get yourself a shrink!' I could never resist having the last word, me. I hadn't bargained on her running though, fast as she did, the boy still bundled up in her arms.

I slipped into Boots and hid beside the nappies. I were having some day of it, no mistake. I were totally out of breath; just trying to breathe normal hurt my chest. I tried to slow down my thumping ticker. The sweat was pouring down me, especially between my breasts. I bought some Tampax Super Plus while I was about it because I was sure my time of month was upon me. Because I always get into trouble with my tongue and strangers around my time of month. I live on me own, so there's nobody to shout at in the house. I used to have a boyfriend and I would rant at him for hours, and one day he just packed his bags and left. I were better off without him anyway because he just got on my nerves. It were only because he had a car that I tolerated him for a bit. It were handy when we did the supermarket shopping. I went out into the street, keeping a sharp eye out for the screaming mother. There are so many mad people in London now. You've really got to watch your back. I know my tongue is going to get me killed by one of those total tulips one day. I think I was already thinking about what I need to do.

I got on the Tube, Piccadilly line. I stared at the faces of the people in the train. Some were reading newspapers, some books, some just staring straight ahead like me. Some had been at work and smelled and were dirty. Some had been shopping. I turned to the girl sitting next to me who looked friendly.

I said, 'You won't believe the day I've had!' I could tell she didn't want me to go into it because she looked panic-stricken. People often look like that when I talk to them as if I'm trapping them or something when I'm only trying to be friendly. I decided to say no more to her. Instead I gave a look, rolling my eyes to indicate my day. She smiled a bit and looked the other way.

I climbed up the four flights of stairs to my council flat in Woodberry Down, off Manor Road. The stairs kill me every time. I switched on the telly when I got into my flat. I can't stand silence all by itself. It was that silly cow that encourages people to slag each other off. The only thing I like about her is that she is fat. I like fat people a whole lot better than thin people. Actually I've noticed a lot of differences between the fat and the thin. The fat are more generous with their cash and their emotions. The thin are more mean and sly. The fat are talkers and the thin are silent. The fat laugh more. The strangest thing of all is when it comes to people who are off their rocker. A thin mad person is worse than a fat one. A thin mad silent type is lethal. Think of all the serial killers and psychopaths and murderers – they've mostly been thin and silent.

Just because I talk a lot people think I'm mad. I hate those silent people that let you talk on and on till you've run yourself into the ground and are left with egg on your face. They leave you repeating yourself while they listen and nod saying their few chosen words because they can choose because they weren't born with the misfortune of having a tongue like mine. I always finish off by saying something stupid like, 'Well I just thought it was out of order,' and when they don't say anything, I say, 'Well I just thought it was out of order,' and then I'll have to trail off because they still haven't said anything. They like their little pauses. I'm always falling into their pauses. They are like traps, or shafts. I fall down into the dark, shouting. It's not the talkers that have the power; it's the silent ones. They're the ones that rule the world. Just look around.

I put the kettle on and make myself a big mug of tea. I open my biscuits and put six on a tea plate for myself. I can't get that woman in the supermarket out of my head. Out of all the trying things today, she's the one that's done my head in. I reckon she was looking in my trolley because she's anorexic or bulimic or something. Well you don't know the half of quiet people; they keep so much hidden.

When I were young most of my friends were shy. I always liked shy people. True, they didn't talk a lot, until they opened up and then there was no stopping them, but they actually liked *me* talking, they liked having me around chatting nineteen to the dozen because I covered for them. Their shyness didn't show if they were with me. If they weren't with me, they'd have to blush and stumble and stuff. But what I really started to notice about the shy was the amount of secrets they had, secrets and grudges and all sorts. I were totally amazed. You'd never imagine how much could be lurking there, under that blushing face, you'd never imagine how much the shy needed revenge. So it makes me wonder about her, that woman. Maybe she told me to see a shrink because she's actually seeing one. You never know. It's possible. Let's face it, it is not normal to go staring for ages into someone's trolley. She were trying to make out that I was the one who weren't normal, but it was her. It was her all along.

Some bloke is screaming at his girlfriend on the telly and the girlfriend is crying and what's-her-face is wandering around with her microphone. What a world. I eat one HobNob after another. I've got so jangled that only my biccies will calm me down. I need a sugar surge or something.

I go into my bathroom and put my tongue out in front of the mirror. It is pink and thick and long and slightly speckled like a bird's egg, but other than that it just looks like an ordinary tongue. You wouldn't suspect it of nothing. I lift it up using my muscles and look underneath the tongue. Again, nothing doing really. A bit gross seeing all the joins of the tongue, stretchy, sinewy, slimy strings. All my life I've been told by so many different people: 'That tongue of yours will get you into trouble one day.' And all my life it has. I'm constantly living on my tongue's edge. I can't afford to take no more risks. Every time my tongue gets me into trouble, it will be punished. Then it will soon learn. I pick up the razor and I cut my tongue. It is actually painful, but the pain feels good. The pain feels deserved. The blood is generous and very red and it pours down my face. I wish they could all see me now.

Timing

I have to get the timing right. Sometimes I do and they don't which leaves me feeling flat and unfortunate. I have grown to depend on the order of things. On a weekday I leave my flat at eight-thirty on foot. I almost always see the first pair – the grandmother and granddaughter. My heart leaps when I see them – the grandmother with her grey straight hair stopping at her neck line, her three-quarter-length navy blue padded raincoat; the granddaughter in her lilac anorak and her blonde spindly hair and her seven-year-old giggle. I often catch it. I never speak to them and they never speak to me. It is enough that I see them at the beginning of the day. Once or twice they've not appeared and I've panicked. They walk towards Didsbury and I walk towards Chorlton along the Barlow Moor Road. We pass right outside the southern cemetery.

I walk down Maitland Avenue and head for Chorlton Water Park. I pass the same little red houses with the same vulnerable, tender front gardens every day. On the corner of Maitland Avenue and Darley Avenue is a cherry blossom tree. In spring its pink is uplifting. I walk down the short steep hill at the entrance to the Water Park. Coming up the hill, as I'm walking down, is the man with his black mongrel. I catch this pair at the end of their walk. The man always tries to whistle his dog, but his whistle has obviously gone – maybe emphysema or something. He makes this breathless whoooo noise at the top of the hill to get the dog to come. Blowing air, a silent whistle. How the dog hears it, I don't know. Do dogs grow tolerant of their owners ageing? Perhaps the dog understands. This man – cap over his bald head, old tweed jacket, slack, loose trousers, slightly stooping back – always nods at me and makes a noise for me too, not hello, but 'Ha' as if long ago he came from a place in a strange forest where the wood people said 'Ha' to each other, as if all people made the same single sound.

I walk down the hill and round the west side of the man-made lake past the avaricious Canada geese and then I see him, the third person. He has his bag of broken bread; I usually catch him at the beginning of the feeding of the geese. These are the geese that would happily destroy all ducks, or snap the fingers of small, round-faced girls. He holds the bread in his hand and they come and snatch it off him. He is a hero. I am frightened of beaks. I dislike the snatch and fury of them. They stretch their too flexible necks, hiss, open their long thin mouths. The violent red inside the beak is horrifying. The cream, criminal stripe at the side of the face. I hate the way they all land at his feet flapping their huge dark wings as if they are clapping. Their tails swish as they make their terrible noise, the honking of the horns. The geese make their dramatic desperate landing just as I am passing. I rush past the goose man thrilled and tense. Then I increase my speed. I walk around the west side of the lake until I come to the stile and then I head for Jackson's Boat Inn, alongside the River Mersey, the river that runs like a long conversation from Manchester to Liverpool. There are golfers out already in their jumpers and shoes. They take a swing at the hard and clever white ball as if they were a new species altogether, old fit men, just landed on the earth somewhere between the first hole and the eighteenth.

It was at the river that I first saw them and, ever since, I've tried to see them again. I've tried coming at the same hour and I've tried coming at different hours. The different hours unsettled me because I missed my grandmother and granddaughter, my no-whistle man, my goose man. I walked past their empty spots with my eyes shut. No amount of tiny white terriers running optimistically along the river-bank or friendly old women and men joined arm in arm, almost surgically joined, who said 'Hello' and 'Lovely day' and nodded, no amount of any of these chance unknown people could compensate for my familiars. So I stopped coming at random hours, early afternoon, late afternoon, early evening, when the pink flush of the sky convinced me again and again that tonight would be the night because the very clouds were wearing highlights in their hair.

I went back to my regular time, leaving my flat at eight-thirty with my flask of orange juice and my soft bread roll with butter and thick-cut old English marmalade to have on the wooden tables outside Jackson's Boat. I never eat breakfast in my flat. It makes me feel too lonely. Other meals I can manage, but not breakfast. I have slept on my own all night. I need to get out and see my familiars.

One of them had bright red copper hair and the other had dark dark curly hair; one of them was wearing a light cream coat; the other was wearing a black fleece; one of them had black skin and the other had white skin; they were both walking along hand in hand when I first saw them in the distance walking towards me. They were just passing the old green bridge that takes you over to the Inn where the Stuart sympathizers used to meet secretly at the time of the Jacobite risings. They would all drink from a bowl of water placed in the centre of the table.

Maybe it was the copper hair that first drew me – she looked Pre-Raphaelite. Then they stopped, quite suddenly, just in front of the green bridge where the fencing narrows the footpath. The copper one threw her arms around the dark one and they kissed at the side of the river. I have never seen a kiss on one of my walks, not a long desperate kiss like that. I had to slow down so that I wouldn't have to pass right by it. It just went on and on and on. The river moaned and rushed and the sun spilled right along the river-bank and this kiss continued. It looked to me, as I walked towards it, like the kiss of the century. It was stunning, compelling. I knew I should look at golfers, but couldn't. I had to pass close to them and hold in my breath in a sort of movement of sympathy. I had to get past them. I couldn't turn back. Who could turn their back on such a kiss? I have not myself had one. A long wet kiss like that. I started to lick my lips quite unconsciously until I noticed myself doing it. Strolling by the river licking my lips. I was about a yard away from them and my footsteps could have been heard, my presence could have been sensed. I walked past them and nobody looked up. I climbed up the stone steps to the old iron bridge. In days gone by I would have had to pay a halfpenny toll to cross this bridge, I thought to myself, clutching at facts to try and remove the impact of the kiss. When was this bridge built? 1816. I turned and looked to my side and the kiss was still going strong. Who was Jackson? Why is the pub called Jackson's Boat? Don't know. Don't know. Don't know. I was hot, sweating. My heart was beating like a bird's. I felt light-headed as if I had gulped a whole gale.

It puzzled me for ages afterwards, the kiss. What was it that thrilled me? Its length? Its public place? The fact that it was two women standing by the River Mersey completely engrossed in each other? The fact that I myself had never had more than a dry peck? It came to me, standing by my kettle waiting for it to boil in my very small kitchen, that witnessing that kiss changed my life. I felt involved, that was it. They involved me. They might not have meant to, but they did. Now they are in my head when I go to bed at night, the dark, dark curly-haired one and the copper-haired one. I kiss them both, gently on the cheek. If I could see them again I would know for sure.

I noticed myself changing in small ways. I am

usually a tidy person. But after the kiss, I left my bed unmade in the morning. I still covered my leftover foods with cling film and cleaned my surfaces with Flash with added bleach and hoovered twice a day. Pine Forest had to be used in the toilet every visit, no matter how small or meaningless. Crumbs, I still could not abide. But general tidiness started to slip after the kiss. I came home and my small pine wardrobe disappointed me, with my white shirts hanging together and my coloured shirts hanging together. After the kiss I mixed up the colour-coding in my wardrobe. Then I went out to buy my supper. I suddenly decided to buy a kebab in that Greek place, Panico's, where I've often seen people queuing. I bought a half bottle of a nice Rioja in Carrington's then I came home and played Strauss's Metamorphosen, crying and sipping my wine. That night, the night of the kiss, I took my clothes off and left them higgedly-piggedly in a heap on my bedroom floor. I went to bed completely naked.

This morning I leave my house at the usual time, eight-thirty. It is raining. Lucky for me the rain never puts off my regulars. The grandmother and granddaughter are on the Barlow Moor Road, a little further up this morning. I have to hang around a while outside the cemetery until they appear, then I continue to walk. The grandmother in her blue padded coat stares at me and looks unsettled. She has given me this look ever since she realized our paths cross every day. Perhaps she dislikes fate. I don't know. How do I know what's inside the old lady's head? She takes her granddaughter's hand and holds it a little too firmly until we've passed each other, silently, meaningfully. One hand on her brolly and the other holding her granddaughter's on their way to school. I wonder which school. There is a school with a strange name just across the Princess Parkway. A school that crouches behind trees where children – which children nobody knows – seem to arrive and depart with nobody witnessing. Perhaps she goes there. I have been tempted to follow them but I know the old lady would be on to me like a shot and would be alarmed. She might even start doing one of those terrible old lady runs where the leg does a semi-circle before it hits the pavement.

I never use an umbrella. If it is raining, I am meant to get wet. Why should I try and avoid the weather's will? Luckily the rain doesn't bother my no-whistle man. He and his mongrel seem to enjoy it. He nods at me and says a louder, 'Ha!' – one he uses for the rain. Of course in Manchester it rains all the time and the people here have a split personality to accommodate it. The bleak, rainy personality and the surprised, sunny one. My no-whistle man is more at home in the rain, evidently. He likes to be able to say to himself, 'Bloody terrible weather today.' He enjoys the feeling that something bad is happening to all Mancunians at once and it makes him complicit with strangers. 'Dreadful eh?' his emphatic 'Ha' says.

The goose man is evidently of the opinion that the geese should not suffer because of the weather. This man, with stick and stooped back, feels obliged to come out, come rain or come shine. His bread is already broken up in the plastic bag. He must break it before he comes out. I noticed after a while that he seems to be able to differentiate one goose from another and that they seem to have some pecking order. Perhaps the geese invented the phrase.

Today I hurry past the goose man, scared as usual. I worry that one of his geese might go after me and peck at the backs of my legs, even though this is quite irrational and they are more interested in bread than leg. I worry just the same and I take a sharp intake of breath as I pass and only let it out when I am round the corner. I know where the fear of beaks is from. My mother had two budgies, one named Yuri Gagarin and the other Martin Luther King. I might have admired the men, but I loathed the budgies. They would be allowed out of their cage to watch *Star Trek* and *Doctor Who*, their favourite programmes. My mother would insist that Martin Luther King sat on my head whilst Yuri Gagarin sat on hers. 'They're just birds,' she'd say. 'Don't be daft.' I hated the soft shifting of light bird feet on top of my fly-away hair. I hated them joining in to the theme tune of *Doctor Who*. I was terrified of bird-do in my hair. The morning Yuri Gagarin was not sitting on his wooden perch inside his cage but lying flat on the floor feet up was a glad morning for me. Martin Luther followed soon after, a heart-broken bird. For three months he carried on bravely, but his budgie chest got less and less puffed and single feathers flew around our brick house in a flurry of grief. One day, the kitchen back door was open and Martin Luther King flew out and never returned. The back door had been open before but the bird had never wanted to go. 'He's gone in search of Yuri,' my mother said, full of understanding. She understood birds but not girls. How could this be? My mother would have been happier with a colourful aviary and no daughter.

I can't say any of our budgies ever pecked my legs or neck, but I lived in fear of them doing so. Each flap, flutter, each sudden bird movement had me breathing soft, fast audible breaths. The goose man is not a great talker, thank God. He never says more than good morning. If he were a garrulous goose man I would be forced to walk in the other direction. Today, in the pouring relentless rain, the geese come untroubled by the weather and take the bread from his hand.

I am convinced I will see them again today, the copper and the dark, because I imagine that the kiss would be even better in the pounding rain, in the biting wind. Exhilarating? I venture to imagine, yes. Love in the rain. Love in the wild, windy north-west rain. I can hear the birds, sheltering in trees, the blackbirds and the song thrushes and the robins and the wrens. I spy a robin redbreast in a small hedge and I take it as a sign that today is indeed the day. The trees look the way they look in spring, like actors waiting for their moment of glory, their drama.

I walk round the edge of the lake and on to the river. The Mersey is moody and morose in the rain; it has lost its ability to rise and swell, to roll over on to the banks and threaten farms and houses. The rain no longer allows the river its excesses. Flood control measures have taken away the natural form of the river. Near Jackson's Boat, the sluice gates open when the level of the river is high and the surplus water runs on to Sale Water Park. At night when I kiss the two of them, the river is in the background. I say to it, 'You too. You've seen the kiss as well.' What has this river not witnessed? What rich mud does this river not know about? My mother used to say to me, when we walked down by the Erskine river near Drymen, 'A river knows, dear. A river knows your secrets.' That terrified me then because I was having bad thoughts about those budgies. I was wishing them dead in their cage. My mother would see the alarm on my face and continue. 'Nothing can be kept secret in a river dear. Secrets rise to the surface and are discovered.'

It might have been the fact that the rain hid her from me or the fact that I was looking into the sulky brown river. But when I look up, I nearly pass out. The rain pours down my face. My hair is soaking wet. I can barely see now. I take my glasses off to wipe the big drops of rain with my handkerchief.

It is her. It is. My heart lurches. I am still holding my glasses in my hand. There in front of me is the dark, dark curly-haired one. Alone. Am I imagining it or is she looking sad? She walks towards me along the muddy river path. Her hands in her pockets. She is as tall as I remember and as dark. Her head is looking downwards. She is wearing her black fleece. I want to rush up to her and say, 'Where is she? What have you done with her?' I want to say, 'I saw you kissing. I've missed you.' She walks by me, but this time she notices me. She notices the colour of my eyes. I know she does. My eyes are my only attribute, the only thing I've got going for me. I keep my glasses in my hand, too vain to put them back on. My hair is too wispy, my nose too sharp, my cheeks lack real definition, but my eyes, kind people have always told me my green eyes are beautiful. I have to do something. I cannot let her pass without speaking. How many people in my life do I let pass without speaking? How often do I go home wishing I had not crushed my own passion? How many times have I sadly opened my fridge and peered inside at the neat contents, the low-fat yoghurts, the bags of red and green lettuce leaves, and felt a crushing despair? When will I let it happen? Why have I kept my lips shut tight? If I let her pass me and do not speak my whole life will be one long regret.

In the past, as a girl, when I was about to say something difficult, I would count down from ten. When I got to zero, I would bottle out and start again at ten. Finally, I'd say the difficult thing I had to say to my mother. My petty admissions of guilt and she'd say, to my absolute horror, 'Are you completely lacking in sensitivity? You have to get the timing right!' I used to repeat this phrase, 'Get the timing right!' but counting down from ten didn't seem to help. Today I don't count. I just take the plunge. I say, 'Hello. No friend today?' And she stares at me as if I am stark raving mad.

Trout Friday

If you want good teeth you must brush your gums as well. Gums cause more tooth loss than tooth decay. That's what the paper said. Melanie went straight to the chemist and bought a brand-new toothbrush. She'd lost too much already and she was only twenty-three and she didn't want to lose her teeth into the bargain. She lost her mother when she was nineteen. She lost her Uncle Barry. She lost a baby she was carrying. She liked it if she could read some fact and act on it. Like she read fish was good for your brain. So now she has salmon Monday, prawn Tuesday, cod Wednesday, haddock Thursday and trout Friday. Weekends she has fish-free because she only really needs her brain during the week. Weekends she splashes out and has takeaway: Peking duck with pancakes, lamb with spicy leaves and nan bread, or Kentucky Fried Chicken with large fries.

So she went straight out of the office, down the High Street and bought a good toothbrush in Boots. Oral B. No point in buying cheap stuff. Who are you cheating? You're cheating yourself. You're cheating your own teeth. In the past Melanie used to brush her teeth at the sink, head down, quick up-and-down movement, final gob. Now she stares in the mirror to see what she is doing. Making sure she doesn't ignore her gums, she brushes in the circular motions she's read about. Not the old up and down she was taught was correct years ago. She makes sure she brushes for the length of time it takes to boil an egg. She has an egg timer in her bathroom. A couple of weeks ago she bought another egg timer because she was getting sick of running up and down the stairs when the timer was in the wrong place. Now she's got two timers. One for the eggs, one for the teeth. As far as she knew the tooth-egg timer never lied. But the egg-egg timer was always letting her down. Often the yellow of her egg would be on the queasy side of runny.

There was her face, her own face in the mirror at night and in the morning. Her mother was from Ireland, County Mayo, and her father was from Trinidad and when she looked in the mirror, the pair of them were behind her, mixing themselves up in her face. Her father's teeth were in her mouth. She hadn't seen him since she was four and could only remember him in the grainy, sketchy images of a fuzzy old film. They definitely weren't her mother's – thank God, because her mother had the most terrible teeth. They were crossed, bless, and quite dark in places. They hadn't stopped her loving her mother, but whenever she had glanced in the direction of her mouth, it had filled her with a nameless worry. A feeling of everything not being right in the world. A sense of unease. So that now the two things were mixed up in her mind: her mother's stained teeth and her mother's dark death. There were her eyes, her father's. A deep dark brown. (Her mother had lovely grey-green Irish eyes, full of the sea, the sky.) And her nose, which was probably a cross between the two: a nostril on either side. There was her mouth, almost comically her mother's; her lips turning down slightly, so that even a smile had an echo of disappointment. Then there were her cheeks, her high cheekbones, that people always admired, that seemed to come from nobody. And her colour which was a mixture of the two. It still struck her as interesting that colour could be blended like that, as if people were paint.

Melanie's skin colour was a perfect mix of her father's very dark black skin and her mother's pale white skin. She'd read somewhere that people with her colour of skin were now being called *beige*. Somehow she didn't like *beige*; it made her think of fashion and clothes. It made her ask questions like: does beige go with khaki? *Beige Britain*. She said, 'No!' out loud when she read that in her magazine. 'Please!' But she didn't like it when one of the girls at work called her *half-caste* because it sounded insulting and she didn't like *mixed-race* because it made her feel muddled. Certainly not *mulatto,* it made her think of mules. Definitely not people who said to her, 'You're neither one thing nor the other.' because that made her feel left out, belonging to nobody. A white woman at a 38 bus stop on Shacklewell Lane had once said to Melanie, out of the blue, in a thick Cockney accent, 'Must be hard for you lot, the blacks don't want you and the whites don't neither. But one day my dear, the whole world will be like you. Just wait and see. You wait.' Luckily the bus came. Melanie bolted upstairs to the top deck. Most upsetting of all, she didn't like it when other black people described her as being *red* or *high yellow* because that made her feel like a primary colour.

On trout Friday, Melanie tended to think about her mother because Friday had been her mother's favourite day of the week. 'When your working week's behind you, darlin',' she'd say to Melanie in the Irish accent she never lost despite living in England for thirty years. Even thirty she said differently. It was more like *tur-ty*, said quite quickly. So Melanie and her mother, Pauline O'Reilly, would have a drink together. And after one drink Pauline would say, 'Look at you! Aren't you beautiful? Aren't you my beautiful daughter? And don't you let anybody tell you otherwise. Do you hear?'

She thought of her father, once a month, on a stuff-your-face Sunday because that was the day her mother told her he had left. 'Just upped and left just like that without a word of warning and after all we'd been through together.' And wasn't heard of or seen again. That is, until yesterday. And then it was most perplexing for Melanie to hear about her father on the day that she thought about her mother. On trout Friday. If she had known the letter was going to be from her father, she would not have opened it until Sunday. It didn't feel right and that was the truth.

Every Friday, she bought her fresh trout at Ridley Road Market in the morning before work. She also bought herself a salmon and cream cheese bagel for breakfast from the twenty-four-hour bagel shop next to the market. (She had once been driven to this shop in the middle of the night and had still found it teaming with bagel people.) Even in the morning the market was already buzzing with all of London, brimming with bright people and boasting shining fruit and vegetables. Early in the morning the market held the promise of the future, a kind of glowing, gleaming optimism, a belief that today was going to be a good day, a sell-all-the-goods day, a leave-little-left-behind day. There were the fruit sellers with their bombastic charm, their lofty language to describe their peaches and oranges, none sweeter or riper. 'These are just perfect, beautifully ripe,' they'd say, loyally, tenderly. Melanie's favourite fruit man liked to shove a grape into her mouth and say 'Try that then,' and wait, standing back a bit, till Melanie said, 'I'll take a pound.' 'Thought you would darlin',' he'd say. 'Pretty girl like you likes a pretty grape.' Melanie liked flirting with the fruit men. The strange rhyming slang they used for money was music to Melanie. It made her laugh when her fruit man shouted things like, 'Mr and Mrs Mustard coming,' to warn another market man of thieves. Hot hands. Peppery.

This early in the day, Ridley Road had no prior knowledge of the distressed, hopeless rubbish and mashed-up fruit and litter that would scatter from the top end of the market to the bottom, from Kingsland High Street to Dalston Lane, by the end of a hard-graft day. No, here it was for Melanie to believe in once more. Brand new. Brimming, bustling, boasting, bragging, black people, white people, poor people, cool people, scary people, soft people. The whole world is here, Melanie thought to herself, looking down the stalls as one carefully piled stack of fruit and veg competed with another for love or money. Melanie liked the market so much she thought of it as a person, bags of personality and generosity. Funnily enough, it reminded her of her mother. 'Variety, Melanie, the spice of life,' her mum would say. Her mother always liked to try things that were different. 'I was a wild one, Mel, couldn't stop me.' Yes, the market was her mother. If Melanie should see her, Pauline O'Reilly, selling six clementines for a pound, or ten big knickers for a fiver or Irish dancing tapes for two pound fifty, she would only be a little surprised.

She smiled to herself and bought three fruits: an apple, a pear and a mango. Mango was good at the market. She'd read somewhere that you should eat three fruits a day and have five portions in total of fruit or veg daily. Since she'd been sticking to this rule rigidly, she'd noticed her dark brown curly hair was looking healthier than usual. It would look even better if she gave up the fags, but she couldn't and that was that. Any articles about smoking and lung cancer, she quickly flicked past, though she was never quick enough to avoid the terrifying headlines MORE WOMEN DYING FROM LUNG CANCER. Headlines like these roared in her face; she'd have to light up to calm down.

She let herself into her office on Kingsland High Street, Dalston Travel, and put her fresh fish in the fridge. (Now, she'd need to make sure not to forget her trout when she was leaving.) She made herself one of her three cups of coffee per day, stirred in two spoonfuls of sugar, the white killer, but what the hell, and sat down in front of her computer with her bagel. Friday was busy in Dalston Travel. Weekends made everybody think of going somewhere. Paris. Amsterdam. Madrid. Lyon. Bologna. Bruges. Brussels. On a Friday, Melanie prepared herself to expect anything.

A couple would come in off the High Street and tell her that they want to spend their New Year watching the aurora borealis. So Melanie would have to be on her toes. The other girls always passed requests like this straight on to her and she took a strange pride in solving these romantic problems for people. 'Well,' she'd say, rubbing her cheek with her finger, 'you've got a couple of options, I can think of. Depends on your purse. How about Tromsø, the most northern city in the world, right close next to the Arctic Circle it is, easy to see the lights. I can do you a three-night package for four hundred and fifty quid each, staying at the Scandic hotel. Or you could try Iceland, fly to Reykjavik then car hire to Fludir, look here,' (Melanie opens a glossy mag at the page) 'easy to see the lights from the walking trails. Do that for six hundred and twenty pounds for five nights including car hire apiece,' she'd smile, triumphantly.

But couples like these always seemed a bit suspicious that their big dream could be planned so easily and could quite often leave without booking anything. One of the girls in Dalston Travel would say, 'What exactly is the aurora borealis, Mel, I mean I've heard of it and that, but I'm not sure.' To which Melanie would reply: 'It's patterns of light across the night sky caused by streams of charged particles from the solar winds.' And the girls would exchange an Isn't-Mel-a-fucking-know-it-all look.

The day was gobbled up in no time at all; soon it would be time for trout. (She had a new trout recipe cut out from a magazine that she was going to try tonight. It looked tasty on the picture, but then they always looked tasty on the pictures, probably the trout were touched up till those little cheeks looked cheeky and plump.) The Friday evening boost to the brain would last until Monday. Since she started with the fish thing, she'd not been making so many mistakes with people's holidays on the computer and she remembered to ask them crucial things like did they want insurance or a vegetarian meal booking; or did they mind getting up at five in the morning to fly home. Perversely, she wasn't actually selling any more holidays since the fish, but she had fewer irate customers and that made a big difference to her at least, if not to her boss.

When people got angry, she'd breathe deeply and say, 'I can see your point, but . . .' and then if they kept on at it, she'd suddenly lose it and end up saying things like, 'No, you're the one that's being rude.' Or, 'Well that's not my problem. You should have told us that.' And once, to the amusement of her colleagues in the agency she shouted down the phone, 'Well fuck off then to Timbuktu.' Her temper was her mother's temper. She'd seen it flare up and burn for a few moments till it smoked and was out. She didn't know what of her personality belonged to her father because she didn't know him, although her mother would often say to her, 'You'rc just like your father, do you know that?' And Melanie would say, 'What do you mean. What do you mean?'

'Oh just wee ways,' her mother would say infuriatingly. 'Tiny wee ways. You're quite picky. He was picky.'

'Picky?' Melanie would say, 'You're pulling my leg!' If only her mother had lived longer so Melanie could have asked her more. Why didn't she make better use of the time. She read somewhere that people who manage their time well suffer less stress. But no matter how well Melanie organized her time, no matter how much time she had alone, her reply, to the, 'All right?' of the girls in Dalston Travel was still, 'I'm stressed out.' Mind you, a lot of them said, 'Me too.' So maybe she wasn't any more stressed than the next woman. 'Rushing's bad for you,' her mum used to say. The way she said it sounded like, 'Russian's bad for you,' and Melanie always pictured her mother walking on the long road away from Moscow. Melanie hadn't travelled that much herself, hardly at all, despite the fact that she got a discount. But she could call up any town or city in the world on her computer and gaze at it: Seville, Innsbruck, Lagos, Leipzig, Dresden, Carcassonne, Lisbon, Freetown, Georgetown, Krakow, Gdansk, Budapest, Bombay, Dehli, Peking. She liked, in the odd free moment, to surf a city. She thought she knew more about travelling than most travellers. She knew the must-sees and the avoids, the dangers and the pitfalls, what to eat and where. She knew the probable weather in every place in the world at any given moment, the political situation, what was happening with the currency. She memorized facts about places and constantly updated the database that was her own mind. A bloke could come into her office in October and say, 'I want something hot for not this Sunday but the Sunday after that to not the next Sunday but the Sunday after that.' And Melanie would say, 'The Canaries.'

The bloke would say, 'What about Greece?'

'Not Greece. Greece isn't hot. You'll be all right with Lanzarote. Here we go, Lanzarote. Self-catering. Two weeks. Three hundred and eighty-nine pounds each.' Each time she booked somewhere, she imagined it for a moment, from the pictures in the brochures and all the travel articles she read in travel sections in newspapers. Pictured the glorious cathedrals, the monasteries, the museos, the Baroque art, the dormant volcanoes, the shimmering sea, the golden beaches, the cobbled streets, the plazas, the statues, the snow-capped mountains, the fountains, the fortresses, the castles and towers and turrets, the ruins, the influence of the Moors, the famous waterfalls, the bubbling mud pools, the flamenco dancing, the snake charmers, the fortune-tellers.

She came home with her fresh trout in her bag (nearly left it in the fridge at Dalston Travel and then remembered it at the last minute – phew.) The letter was lying there waiting in the hall. It wasn't airmail so there was nothing to warn her, except that Melanie didn't get all that many letters and most of the ones she did get she was already expecting. Here, in the hall was an unexpected letter. She picked it up and climbed up the stairs till she got to her one-bedroomed flat. She unlocked her door and put the letter down on the kitchen table. An unexpected letter could not be ripped open straightaway; that would not be so pleasurable. When she'd finished her trout she would open it. It could be from the father of the child she lost wanting her back. The writing on the envelope looked a bit like his. Well, he could take a running jump, she thought, turning on her oven. Jump high, boy. No way was she going down that road again. Fingers burnt. She was just getting herself back together from it all; and even now, with her new regime, she could still find herself sobbing in bed at night thinking about her lost baby and what she would have called her and whose teeth she would have had and whether or not she would have had her eyes. Intuition had told her it was a girl.

The ripped out page from the magazine sat next to the letter on the table. The recipe was called *Trout en Papillote.* Melanie didn't have a clue what that meant but she fancied doing something different for a change. Most times, she grilled or fried or steamed or baked the fish – salt, pepper, that was it. This recipe was for two people but she'd have to adapt that. All the way through cooking her trout, she was reminded of the fact that she was eating alone, halving the ingredients of the recipe.

She brushed the foil with olive oil, and then she lay her solitary Friday trout across it, diagonally. She seasoned the fish with sea-salt flakes and black pepper and put two sprigs of thyme in its cavity. Then she brought the foil up around the fish like the magazine said leaving an opening to pour the liquid into. This was fun. Everything was going to plan. She poured some white wine and olive oil and two teaspoons of lemon juice – her mum would have been proud of her cooking proper like this – into the parcel. Then she sealed up the parcel like a secret or a letter and put it into the oven to bake for 13–15 minutes. At this point the egg timer came in handy, she used it three times and a half because her watch was wonky.

Now to the tomato, olive and chilli salad. She was beginning to feel quite the sensation in her small kitchen cooking cordon bleu for herself like this. She felt in perfect control. Graceful. Elegant. Something was missing though. Her sounds. She put on Coldplay and pressed the track called 'Yellow'. She liked that song. She played it over and over again while her trout cooked that Trout Friday. The words were about her; she imagined him singing them straight at her. She cut her tomatoes into wedges and arranged them on one small plate. She sprinkled chilli and garlic and drizzled olive oil and scattered with olives. 'And it was all yellow,' she sang at the top of her voice. She sang in perfect pitch, which was more than she could say for the lead singer of Coldplay. She sprinkled chopped parsley over her salad. It would be nice to be cooking for her mother. Why did her mother die before she could cook one proper, special meal for her? The trout would be ready. She rushed to the oven, feeling slightly harassed now in case her fish was going to fall to pieces and collapse. This often happened when she cooked fish; she'd end up swearing Fuck, Fuck, Fuck, at the top of her voice because she had promised herself she wouldn't overcook the fucking fish. And then she went and did. Better to have it near-raw like the Japanese. The Japanese have the lowest rate of heart disease in the world. Her mum wouldn't have liked sushi though. Pauline O'Reilly wasn't a raw-things fan.

Each person can open his or her own parcel, the recipe said. That meant her. She could open her own parcel. She sat down at her table set for one. She dished some of the tomato and chilli salad on to her plate. (She had not bothered with the chunky chips cooked in olive oil, too fattening.) Then she remembered the letter. Her little trick of trying to deliberately forget the letter while she cooked had worked.

Before she opened her parcel of fish or her letter, she rushed up to the bathroom and pee'd. Then she put on some chocolate brown lipstick so that she could feel that she had really made an effort and she couldn't tell herself otherwise. She looked in the mirror and smacked her lips together. Every time she looked in the mirror, she asked herself the question as if for the first time: Am I beautiful or am I plain? People told her she was beautiful. Men whistled at her and bothered her, particularly black men, but she still didn't feel beautiful. Well, not entirely. God! The trout! She flushed the toilet quickly, washed her hands and rushed to sit down at her small table and eat.

A letter from her father on Trout Friday. She opened it with her clean fish knife. His letters were big and long and sloped to the right. The paper was lined, narrow feint and small. The letter was a page and a half. Melanie took all this in, the blue ink, the blotches, the words crossed out before she read it. It was not dated, but there was an address. What a turn up for the books. What would her mum say if she were here? She wished she were. She wished she could say, 'You'll never guess who I've just heard from. Out of the blue.' All this time she'd thought he was living in Trinidad or Tobago, all this time she'd looked at pictures of the beautiful beaches of Tobago on the Internet and priced the hotels, he was actually living up the road in Tottenham. Townsend Road, Tottenham. 'No!' she squealed as she took in the address.

The letter said he was sorry to hear her mother had died. Only just heard! Yet the news was four years old. He said he wanted to meet her and see what she had turned into and maybe she could cook him a nice meal. Melanie clapped her hands. 'Oh that's rich,' she said aloud. 'That's really rich.' She opened up her silver foil parcel. She was determined not to let the letter spoil her trout. She slid it out of the foil carefully and on to her plate. It was perfect, silver and pink and blue. It looked so beautiful she didn't want to eat it. She gently pulled it open and took out the bone. She put the weak floppy skeleton on a side plate. A few stray bones still stuck to the flesh. She picked them off one by one. She was not keen on fish bones. Some people ate them, but not Melanie. She cut the succulent flesh carefully and took her first mouthful. Though she said it herself her *trout en papillote* was delicious. 'Take a running jump,' she said, as she thoughtfully tasted her tomato and chilli salad. Her mouth was alive and tingling with the sensation of her own cooking. She looked down at the letter while she ate, reading it again and again to see if there was something she had missed. He did sign off: *Love Dad.* Calling himself, Dad, struck a false note; although he was her father, he hadn't earned the name, Dad. It didn't sound real, it sounded pretend.

It occurred to her that if she met up with her father, she might discover what her mother had meant by 'picky'. She considered this for a minute. Fussiness can be passed down, she'd read somewhere. There is even a shy gene. But she didn't want to know. Melanie didn't want to know what was her and what was him. She tried to remember her father from that blurry childhood memory, to zoom in and enlarge him. But the only thing she could see clearly was his hand, his black hand, his clearly defined dark life-lines, his quite lovely nails. She took her last bite of trout. She struggled for a minute trying to imagine her father sitting opposite her eating dinner with her. Would he mind her having a glass of wine? In a way, the picture of Melanie and her father at dinner was quite romantic, but something made her shudder. Something repelled her. It was too late, somehow, to have dinner with her father. 'Nah,' Melanie said to herself, 'Leave him like that. Leave it out.' She poured herself another glass of white wine. It was crisp, cold, elegant. She tried to think of more wine words she had read. Fruity. Buttery. Bold.

The woman with fork and knife disorder

Her name was still Irene Elliot, the same Irene Elliot who had been drying her dishes and putting them away for years. She was quick, didn't even notice what she was doing. Second nature where things went: the cups and saucers, the pans, here, the dinner plates, there, the tea plates up there. The daughter, Mary Ann, was at high school the day it first happened. The fork and knife drawer was open. The clouds had broken up, gone off their separate ways. The sun was filtering in through the kitchen windows, sliced through the blinds.

She was humming to herself in a way that was not unlike thinking odd thoughts. She went to put a knife in the knife bit and it slipped out of her hand and joined the spoons. 'Silly Irene,' she said to herself. She had always had this habit of naming herself aloud as if she were outside herself, a character. (How could you make yourself real?) You could have knocked Irene over with a feather when I heard, she'd say to Sandra over the fence. Or, Irene will just have a cup of tea to herself. 'Silly Irene,' she said and took the knife out and placed it in the knives bit.

A moment later the same happened with a dessert spoon. Somehow, it upset the forks. For a split second, Irene felt uneasy. Her attention must be slipping. (What makes attention slip?) She was one of those women who got angry easily. If she forgot something she should have remembered, the name of the place where she'd been staying on holiday. If she left something behind; if she dithered at a crossroads. If a word wouldn't come to her, she would get into a tight-lipped fury, a sharp anger. She sighed and kept her eyes peeled on the cutlery drawer. Still a fistful of knives and forks and spoons to put away. *Dizzy, Dozy, Irene.*

She was humming, *I gave my love a cherry it had no stone. I gave my love a chicken it had no bone.* Irene used to sing that to Mary Ann when she was a wee lassie: now that Mary Ann was a wee lassie no more she loathed her mother singing. Apparently Irene's voice trembled too much. When Mary Ann was out, she sang. Who would have believed her girl, her lovely girl, who used to worship her, follow her around and look at her with such devotion, such love in her big wide childhood eyes, could find so much of her revolting. As if Mary Ann hated her – but the worst thing was that part of Irene could not resist seeing herself through Mary Ann's teenage eyes. It was a strange close thing living alone with her adolescent daughter. The smallest of movements could annoy daughter dear. A simple thing like drying her hands on her apron infuriated Mary Ann. Even the sight of the apron incensed her. 'Nobody wears aprons anymore, Mum,' Mary Ann would say. 'I do.

I like my pinnie,' Irene would say back, knowing in the small, sick, glad bit of her heart that this reply would make Mary Ann seethe. Or when she kissed her lips together after putting lipstick on and made a tiny phut-phut noise. Mary Ann thought Irene was overweight, she could tell. Too much on the hips, the thighs. Double chin. Fat arms. Whenever they were going out somewhere, rare these days, Mary Ann would look Irene up and down in such a way that made Irene uncomfortable for she could hear her daughter's bad thoughts.

When Iain left (though *left* was hardly adequate – when Iain split up their home, when Iain took an axe to their house, a machete to their marriage, when Iain abandoned them, when Iain cut loose, cut adrift, cut the knot, severed the tie, when Iain broke up their family), Irene could tell Mary Ann thought it was all Irene's fault.

The last time Irene hugged her daughter, Mary Ann's body went rigid and hard, fighting against her. Her daughter's muscles – tensed up and hateful. It was odd to consider that Irene had actually given birth to a girl who would turn on her like this. In her darkest moments, Irene was upset with her own body; it had clearly betrayed her; it obviously had a hand in the matter. 'It'll pass, Irene,' she told herself. Irene didn't remember ever being like this to her own mother when she was a teenager. She remembered having the odd bubble and greet when she got her period, but that was the hormones definitely. With Mary Ann, Irene couldn't put her hand on her heart and say that it was the hormones. Part of her, it seemed, had just been waiting, ever since she turned, what, nine? Was that fair? Were families fair?

When she looked down, everything was in a terrible state. Four of the knives were splayed across the forks. Two of the forks were lying with the spoons. Five of the spoons had joined the knife section. Some teaspoons were on the edge of the forks. Exasperated, irritated, a little edgy. 'Bother,' she said and when she saw that the sharp knife was lying, serrated edge staring into her face, she said, 'Bugger.' She assumed her head was wandering and that was that. (Where did it go, did it wander back, lost, over the years?) She took the wrong cutlery out and put it back where it was supposed to go. All the spoons lay gleaming inside one another. The knives lay on their sides flat and passive. Everything was neat, properly sorted. In the right place.

Maybe she wouldn't have thought anything of it if the same thing hadn't happened a week later. She went to put a knife away in the knife section. When she next looked down that same knife had somehow cut loose and joined the teaspoons, lying blatantly across them, almost smiling, a wide silver smile. That was when, looking back, that was the moment, the turning moment, when she felt as if someone had stuck a carving knife into the side of her ribs. She was frightened. She dropped the whole lot of cutlery on the floor. It made a terrible racket like screeching music in a horror movie. Clattering and crashing on to her kitchen tiles. It seemed to go on and on and on as if she had a whole canteen in her hands. She rushed upstairs, pulling herself up, her two hands clutching the banister, closed her bedroom curtains, yanked back her covers and she went to bed and she cried.

Of course the daughter came home and wanted to know what was going on. A pile of cutlery on the floor, no dinner, her mother in bed. Irene knew better than to tell her that the forks and knives were acting up and had a mind of their own and that she couldn't get them to lie in their right place. She told her that she had a pain in her left side and had had to lie down. Mary Ann scowled, a look that was the double of her father's scowl, so close, the same craggy, jagged face, the cheeks hollow and sharp with anger, the chin jutting out righteously, that it was as if he was standing just behind her. It made her gasp.

Mary Ann's eyebrows worked themselves into a hateful state. She didn't like her mother having mysterious pains. She didn't believe in her pains. Whenever Irene said any simple thing to Mary Ann like, 'My head's tight, screws fastening into me,' or 'My stomach has got a small man inside, chewing,' or 'My chest has a snake wrapped round and round stopping me from breathing properly,' anything like that, the daughter froze. Mary Ann nodded slowly, chewing, with her skirt too high and her knees like scrubbed round potatoes.

That evening, Irene sent Mary Ann out for fish and chips from the fish shop. They looked so reassuring when they came back wrapped in their hot paper, the smell so comfortingly fishy, so reliable. Nice light batter. Vinegar. Plenty salt. Big mug of tea. Nothing like a fish supper, Irene said. Mary Ann ate hers straight from the paper, 'that's the whole point.' Irene put hers on a warm white plate she'd preheated in the oven. She ate hers with a knife and fork. Mary Ann tore at hers with her bare fingers. 'Fingers were made before forks,' she said, in her dead-pan teenage voice which hardly ever went up or down. 'So they were!' said Irene as if this was a revelation to her.

Irene took a deep breath, then said airily to Mary Ann–

'It's you for the drying, me for the washing.'

'What? I hate drying. It's stupid. Let them drip.'

'I'm wanting the place tidy. I want everything put away.'

'Tidy for what? Nobody's coming.'

'Does everything have to be an argument with you?'

'You make me argue.'

'Just dry the bloody dishes!'

'I hate putting cutlery away.'

'Do you? Do you?' Irene moved closer towards her. 'Why?'

Mary Ann shrugged. 'Don't get all excited. I just hate it. It's boring.'

Irene watched from the corner of her brown eye, Mary Ann putting all the knives and forks in their right place, no bother. They watched a bit of telly together, *The Royle Family.* They didn't speak much. Mary Ann didn't like talking when the telly was on.

Irene woke up at seven-thirty to wake Mary Ann who was big enough to wake herself but never did. The daughter was even worse first thing in the morning. Never looked pleased to see her mother, or the day. 'What time is it?' she growled. 'Why didn't you get me up sooner? I'm going to be late now.' She pushed past Irene into the shower, slamming the door. Irene shrugged. Why couldn't she yawn pleasantly and say good morning Mum and maybe give her a bit of a kind look, a smile? It was awful this. To feel this constant hatred fuming away, already up and steaming first thing in the morning. You would think animosity might need a roll or a coffee or something to get going.

Down the stairs she went to put the kettle on, holding on to the banister again. Already rattled, uneasy, she felt she was living on a knife-edge. She was wearing her Chinese caftan dressing gown that Mary Ann thought was hippyish and embarrassed her in front of her friends. And her oriental slippers. She liked occasionally buying things that bit different. Not the same as the rest of the flock. A splash of colour and country. She picked up her *Glasgow Herald* and brought in her pint of milk and padded towards the kitchen. As soon as she opened the door, she knew something had happened. Slowly, she walked to the blinds and pulled them open. The daylight peered anxiously through the spaces. She filled the kettle, put it on. She put some bread in the toaster and went to get out a knife to butter it. That was when she gasped. The knives were all missing. There were no knives in the drawer at all. The forks were there like a bunch of strange people missing their spouses. The spoons were there, still sleeping. The teaspoons were at the top where they should be. Irene picked up a spoon and stared into it. Her distorted reflection loomed in the spoon, upside down. She stared at herself in the spoon for a terrible moment, transfixed. Her face looked quite long and thin.

She rushed up the stairs and barged into the bathroom. The lock didn't work properly and could easily be forced. Mary Ann was still steaming in the shower and the room was thick with mist. Irene Elliot coughed as Mary Ann's steam fingered her throat. She waved her arms around dramatically in the fug. Mary Ann covered her breasts with her arms and crossed her legs together to try and hide her body. 'You can't barge in here like this. What's going on?' Mary Ann wrapped herself in a white towel and swept out of the steam into her bedroom, banging the door shut. What was this thing with banging doors? What did it mean? It meant she wasn't supposed to go in, but what else? Mary Ann did it so much she almost became the closed door. Her face looked like it, shut and wooden. There was no give in her face anymore. When she was a wee girl she used to look up and there was so much give, so much enthusiasm spread all over her small cheeks. Gone now. Who was she, this girl that swept out of the bathroom and banged her door on her? Irene breathed slowly to herself. Mary Ann did not go downstairs, that was certain. She couldn't have gone down or else Irene would have seen her. Irene returned to the kitchen. When she opened the drawer, the knives were all there again as plain as day. 'Oh Jesus, Irene,' she said. 'Irene's going to have to see somebody.'

Mary Ann came clattering into the kitchen with her big gangly teenage self. 'Why did you barge in on me like that?' 'I don't know. I forget.' Irene said hesitantly, laughing a silly, breathy laugh. 'You forget!' Irene could hear Iain's coldness. She had borne a daughter that had turned out to be her husband. She knew it in her bones. The way her daughter talked to her cut deep. Now that she loathed him, she partly loathed her for being him, for being so like him, so snide and superior. It was a terrible feeling – to suspect her own daughter of being her husband.

Irene Elliot made an appointment to see her GP, Doctor Aspinall. Two days' time – Thursday morning. Mary Ann had left for school banging out of the house. The minute she went, Irene sighed with relief. She felt lonelier when Mary Ann was at home, more strange to herself. There were too many things Irene didn't know and Mary Ann cruelly enjoyed pointing them out. Clever and arrogant, like father like daughter. Irene had never been clever. Clever people frightened her and bored her almost to death. If she happened to get stuck in a conversation with one of them, caught unawares, she felt herself seize up and all language leave her. She didn't like people who asked her what she thought of such and such. The new Labour government, what was going on with the white farmers of Zimbabwe, the situation in Sierra Leone, what to do with paedophiles. It all alarmed her. Nor did she like to be asked which painters or writers or singers she liked. Mary Ann had a clever friend home with her once who asked her if she'd read *The Catcher in the Rye* or if she'd read *Catch 22*. 'No,' Irene replied, 'but I've heard the expressions.' Mary Ann's friend looked blankly through her, it seemed, as if beyond Irene there was another world. Mary Ann burned, her cheeks took on a glow not of embarrassment, but of anger. Clever people made Irene Elliot feel trapped and claustrophobic. She couldn't wait to escape their talk in her ears. It was exhausting for her trying to concentrate, trying to take in what was being said and remember things. Clever people liked to show off their knowledge, they were never content just acquiring it, they had to bang on and on about it. Irene was never a show off.

She went into the kitchen to make herself a coffee. She steeled herself. Mary Ann was out so it wouldn't happen. She was sure it was something to do with Mary Ann. She opened the cupboard and pulled out the jar of Maxwell House coffee. The lid was open and a spoon was sticking out of it. She opened the fridge for the milk and it all fell out of the fridge, slashing, stabbing, smashing on to the floor. The knives, the forks, the spoons, the carving knife, the bread knife, the fish knives, the steak knives, the meat cleaver, the soup spoons, the dessert spoons, the serving spoons, the ladle, the potato peeler, the potato masher, the knives, the forks, the spoons. 'Knife, fork, spoon. Knife, fork, spoon,' she said as she picked them all up. 'Knife, fork, spoon, soup spoon, teaspoon, that's a fish knife!' she cried out triumphantly. 'That's a steak knife!' she screamed. She switched it around, flick-flick, as if it was a sword. 'This is a fork!' said in a low, slow voice. She was sweating. There was sweat between her cleavage, under her arms, between her legs, in the join of her arms, under her double chin. She ran a basin of hot water and put some Fairy Liquid in. She threw the entire set of cutlery in there and let it sink like her heart. 'She's not going to get me this way. There's nothing to be done except carry on, Irene,' she said aloud. 'Get this washed, dear, and put it away.' She took the sponge with the green crust on it and scrubbed. A small sharp knife sliced open the tip of her thumb. She stood quite detached watching her blood swim among the knives and forks and spoons. She felt dizzy as if part of her was falling away, as if her womb was loose or some organ had floated free of everything else inside her. Her mouth filled with saliva and she swallowed fast trying to keep the sea in. Her eyes were watering furiously and it was as if somebody was inside her stomach pulling the ropes, letting the boat out. She heaved and rocked and threw up into the basin with the blood and the forks and the spoons and the knives.

She had to go upstairs; she had to lie down. This short journey upstairs clutching the banister was becoming so desperately familiar. If she could just get horizontal, she might be safe. She washed her face in her bathroom with a cold flannel. Her hair was sticking to her scalp. She was hot. She took off her blouse and her skirt and her stockings and she lay down on her bed in her pants and her bra.

Sleep opened its jaws and let her in. Her dreams when Mary Ann came barging into her bedroom were still there and if Mary Ann hadn't been so urgent, she might have been able to grip them. There was a deaf girl who didn't want her to write a note in capital letters; there was a boat, the bottom slashed, leaking water; there was a man who ejaculated into the choppy sea with Irene Elliot watching. There was so much of it, creamy, frothy, she was quite enthralled. It mixed with the froth of the sea, the high, wailing tip of the waves. It was windy, salty. The man's hair flew about his face. She was just trying to snatch more of him, to remember who he was, when Mary Ann came in.

The daughter surprised Irene then. She sat down on the edge of her bed; she put her hand on her forehead. 'Mum,' she said in a really kind tone, such a lovely kind tone that Irene could have fallen happily asleep to it, 'Mum. You're not well. You need to go to the doctor. I'll clean it up. Don't worry. Shall I call the doctor out?' Mary Ann asked.

'No, I've got an appointment for tomorrow.' Irene felt the tears in her come from a long way: across a mountain, sliding down a hurrying waterfall, along by a babbling brook. Finally they caught up with her and she heaved and rocked – Mary Ann at her side saying, 'Don't, Don't get in such a state, Don't. It's probably a virus or something.' Irene laughed in the middle of her sobs happy that Mary Ann seemed to care. She sniffed and smiled. The snot ran down Irene's face and Mary Ann rushed up to get some toilet paper, hurrying back into the room with a big wad of it wrapped round her wrist like a bandage.

Doctor Aspinall always stood up as a patient entered his room. He sat back down when they were seated. 'So, Mrs Elliot, what's the problem?' (The problem? Where to find the containers for problems.) The doctor smiled with a pained expression on his face. Not a genuine smile, Irene thought. It looked as if it was hurting his face, false and stretchy. 'How can I help?' he looked up again, trying to swallow his irritation. He had a lot of patients outside still waiting to see him.

'I've been having trouble with my cutlery,' Mrs Elliot said tentatively.

'Oh yes?' He tried to keep his head down looking at the prescription pad, his hand seemed as if it was itching to write. A bloody lethal dose of morphine. 'This is a new one on me. Go on. I'm intrigued.' Doctor Aspinall smiled a small smile.

'When I go to put the forks and knives in the right place, my hand just can't,' Mrs Elliot stabbed around for the right word, 'how can I put it? Well it just won't organize itself to do it right.' Organize was not the right word. 'I can't co-ordinate myself,' she said, seizing on this word *co-ordinate*. 'It's as if I've got two different sides and they won't work together. Then yesterday I went to get a spoon for my coffee and the cutlery fell out of the fridge, every last fork, and I didn't put it there. I know I didn't put it there. My daughter denies it as well. It's just too much. It's all too much. And a lot of it is very sharp and dangerous. My husband liked sharp cutlery, so that it would cut his steak properly. A lot of our knives have those jaggedy edges.'

Doctor Aspinall stared at something on the wall just beyond Mrs Elliot. Irene actually turned uneasily and looked at the spot behind her.

'I'm going to be frank with you, Mrs Elliot. This knives and forks business is beyond my ken. I'll have to recommend for you to see another doctor.'

'I hope you don't mean a psychiatrist?' Mrs Elliot said anxiously. 'I think I'm just tired. Maybe my mind is playing tricks on me.'

'Well let me prescribe some Prozac and see how we go with that. If it happens again, you come back and see me. It could be a problem with your brain. A left side, right side thing.'

'A problem with my brain?' Mrs Elliot echoed, impressed. As far as she was concerned there had always been problems with her brain. Her brain wouldn't do what she wanted it to do. She could feel the limitations of her own mind. She'd always been able to feel them. Like shutters coming down. Like blinds blocking out the light. But sometimes she wanted to know things like who first thought of putting a buttercup under somebody's chin to see if they liked butter. 'Yes, a brain scan would maybe not be a bad idea.' Doctor Aspinall repeated looking back down at his prescription.

It made Irene Elliot wonder at herself. What was it like inside her brain? What activities were taking place? How busy was her brain? Was her brain like her mother's brain – her mother was always called harebrained, like Irene. Or was it like her father's brain? Her father was tall and bald and supposedly brainy. He had the bold walk of the very bright, quite a surprising long stride.

The very next week Irene was back, sitting in front of Doctor Aspinall who was sitting behind his desk.

Could you just give me a check up? It's been happening again. Could you just listen to my heart? Somehow, it seemed that if the doctor listened to her heart, he would know it was broken. This time, Doctor Aspinall insisted on recommending her to a psychiatrist, who for all he knew, he added ruefully, might be a specialist on people with knives and forks disorder. Irene suddenly felt excited. 'You mean other people have it?'

'Noooo. Just a joke,' the doctor said and gave Irene a look that suggested humour was lost on the mentally ill.

Doctor Aspinall gave Irene a number to ring – 'a very sympathetic woman called Jenny Spence.' He himself would be ringing her to pass on the details of her case. He also increased the strength of her Prozac prescription. Irene returned home. The light was strange in her street; Kenmuir Drive looked different to her now. Her whole street was full of sadness, hidden behind the curtains. She knew it for certain now. Her own unhappiness allowed her to see everybody else's. She counted the pavement slabs till she got to her own number like a child. Everybody lived behind a hedge or a fence or a gate or a post. Each neighbour was neatly divided from the next. The hedges were too neatly trimmed, completely flat on top. Most of the houses were well painted. A dowdy dirty house stood out. Most of the houses had blinds. A house with just curtains looked poor. The borders of the small suburban gardens were full of sad little flowers, pansies and geraniums, everyone making their best effort, but no flair or imagination. It seemed outrageous that she should possess a key to a door to a house that meant nothing to her. She stared at her own key dumbly before opening the stranger's door. She nearly passed out.

All along her narrow hall corridor, cutlery was laid out as if many people were expected to a banquet on her dark maroon carpet. All places set, but wrongly. Even Irene could see that. Some places were all spoons. Some all forks. Some with knives across the top and teaspoons down the sides. A lot of cutlery was in the middle of the hall, laid out at intervals. Irene had forgotten that she owned half of it. A silver ladle. A huge serving spoon with a marble handle. Some African salad servers, wooden, that Iain had brought back from somewhere whose name she can't remember. Proper napkins; white and rolled in their holders, that she never used these days, were at each place in various positions, some on the top, some at the left, some at the right. Irene thought she saw one of the napkins float for a minute and then drop. Her first impulse was to straighten things out. Lay things out properly. The whole hall was as big a challenge as any she had had in recent weeks. It was a matter of putting the right bit in the right place. There was faint music playing in the background. A fine, airy, elegant waltz.

Irene stood up and waltzed down her hall. *One*, two, three. *One*, two, three. Pas de bas. Pas de bas. She had to be careful not to stand on any of the cutlery. Her feet had to be as dainty as someone born with a silver spoon in her mouth. Iain was a dauntingly good waltzer. Irene was adequate. When

Irene watched Iain with women who really could waltz, graceful and nimble, straight backs, long legs, pretty noses turned up in the air to the music, she knew that Iain felt as if he had a wife that didn't work properly. Like a clock that didn't keep time. Irene would lose the beat in her head after just a few turns. Concentrate! Iain would whisper into her ear, viciously, steering her body with his overly masculine arms. *One*, two, three. Listen. Can you not hear the beat, woman? But that would only make matters worse. Irene felt her steps disintegrate into a slow shoe shuffle, a scramble, one foot desperately chasing the other to the same silly spot. Until she had to put her hand across her head and wipe the sweat from her brow – no one else seemed to sweat – and say, 'I'm deadbeat, dear. Have a dance with Iris Murray.' Iain would settle her down somewhere and go off and that would be that. He wouldn't ask her to dance again until it was all over. *One*, two, three. *One*, two, three. The music got louder. Knife fork spoon.

Suddenly Irene was seized by an overwhelming desire to take a sharp knife and stab it into her heart. The desire was so strong she could almost see herself doing it. A stab, a slash, a sharp slit; a cut, a chop, a slice. All of them so tasty. If she could just mark herself, one creative cleave with the carving knife. Rip her own useless, pathetic skin till it split, till she was wounded, till everything burst forth from the gash. If she could rock her own foundations, rupture herself. It was so exhilarating the picture, the temptation to do herself this final harm. Her mouth was dry. Her eyes steady on her own flesh. One part of her was crying out to shred herself, to make mincemeat. She could visualize the dynamic and dramatic red of her own blood, sputtering, stuttering, saying see, see, see, I told you so. Out of the pit of her black handbag, she pulled the number of the Spence woman. It felt like calling 999. Her fingers trembling and hovering above the numbers until they punched them out, one by one. She felt as if she might explode by her own telephone into a mass of tiny wires and veins and bones. Out of breath. She could not still herself. A voice came on, a recorded voice, friendly, asking for a name and a time and a number. Irene forgot her own number; she could never remember anything under pressure. The phone went into its handset on its own, it seemed. Irene let out a huge, windy sigh. Outside the wind was slicing the trees, clipping the grass, snipping the hedges.

The cutlery in the hall was set for the banquet. Mary Ann would deal with the guests. That one could be sociable with other people if it suited her. Quite the charmer, like the father. For a moment, she couldn't think who could be coming. Most of the joint friends had plumped for Iain after the separation. All the folk she had cooked for, dinner after bloody dinner. They had all branched off. They'd followed his swallowtail. That life went, just like that. Life was puzzling. Friendships that seem detailed and trusty enough, that seem to have accumulated enough intimacies, knowledge about each other's likes and dislikes, that evaporated into nothing. What was she to make of them? What was she to have thought about her life? Was it real at all? Or was it all fake, sham, pretence. Oh all the hugs in the hall when leaving. Oh all the, 'That was lovely, Irene. You excelled yourself.' All a load of hooey. Baloney. Shimmy shammy. Pointless, empty talk. Nobody meant a single word of what they said. Flannellers. Lying, cheating, false teeth. None of those joint friends that had shared the Sunday joint of lamb or beef, or gone on joint holidays, none of them so much as phone her now or drop by to see how she is. There was the fork in the road and off they went in husband's direction. It was beyond belief. The people she had never been all that close to moved forward. They surprised her with their kindness and support. They were a revelation. The ones that she expected nothing from.

Into the kitchen she went and pulled from the fridge a free-range, corn-fed, yellowing chicken. She put rosemary on it. Some lemon juice, some olive oil, and she shoved it straight into the oven to roast. She went to peel some potatoes, but there was no peeler. She found it in the hall, posing as a soup spoon. It would have to be plain fare. She was never much of a cook anyway, not even when she tried cooking lamb couscous or Chicken Karachi. All of her efforts tasted the same – spicy stews that made pleasant guests' eyes water. Plain fare was best. Her grandmother from Lochinver liked nothing but plain fare. Plain fare for rosy cheeks, she used to say. Carrots. Parsnips. Onions. Irene hadn't known she was giving a dinner. She went upstairs to lie down while the cowardly chicken cooked. This was the parting of ways. Bed, bed, bed. She could lay a wreath on her bed. She could plait her auburn hair and lie down next to her wreath. All she felt like these days was sleep. Sleep the great I am. Sleep the great pretender.

Forty winks. Why was she tired like this all the time? Never able to sleep properly. Too jangled and jumpy. It was as if Mary Ann belonged to a different life now. The day was so long it seemed like a journey. Mary Ann's malice, temper, sulleness, slyness was far away. Hazy. A scowl over the hills. Irene wanted to die. Let Mary Ann go and live with her father. She had been asking why she couldn't. Well let her fuck off and go and live with him, Irene shrieked to herself, enjoying the shock of swearing inside her own head. Fuck off, she said again. Just fuck the fuck off.

Irene had been tempted to tell Mary Ann that Iain didn't want her either, but she had managed to stop herself. She got up. At least Mary Ann could have a nice dinner when she came in. She had her own key. The wind whispered and hooted like an owl. All along Kenmuir Drive the bushes and the plants and the flowers shook and trembled. The sky was aghast and drained and serious as if it had just been through a long illness.

What would Jenny Spence want her to tell her? Irene walked quickly in the wind with no hat, no scarf, with her thin cream raincoat, no brolly. She remembered as a child digging in her bit of back garden, which was all earth then, no grass yet, digging with a spoon in a pair of tartan trousers and red wellingtons. Digging for fat juicy worms, translucent and other-worldly. The dirt under her small nails, the earth in her tiny, trusting fingers. She walked to the end of her own street and down to Calder Street. She would go to the park. She would go to the park and have a coffee and feed the ducks. She would make herself sane doing a sane thing. She could feel herself split. It wasn't like people said, this feeling of madness. She was not out of her head. She was in her head too much. Part of her knew what she was doing and knew it was bad; but the other part couldn't stop her. She just couldn't stop her. She didn't want to stop her. She wanted to go all the way. To cut herself in two. Knife and fork.

The photograph that was still on their mantelpiece – why didn't she take it down? Did she think he'd come back, did she think she'd have him back? – of Iain and Irene on their wedding day, cutting the cake. Both hands holding the knife.

Irene had spoiled their tenth wedding anniversary when Iain took her to a posh restaurant in Callander and they had a four-course meal and Irene started eating from the inside out. From the minute she had sat down that time, she knew things were going to go wrong. Just the sight of all of the cutlery made her anxious. She didn't like fancy places really, all the hush and seriousness about the food. She was more comfortable in the restaurant inside Littlewoods. She never knew what to say or do. Iain coloured and then hissed, 'The other way for Christ sake.' For some reason, Iain always thought himself superior to Irene even when it came to sitting down and eating a dinner. Irene's napkin always slid off her knee and on to the floor. Iain's napkin would never do that. Well perhaps Iain had more practice since his job involved more and more fancy dinners. He was a long way from the Gorbals boy she had fallen in love with. This Iain had acquired all these particulars.

She got to the park. The café was quite busy – despite the bad weather. Irene hoped she didn't look strange. She was sure it must show on her face. Her top lip hesitated on the bottom. She ran her tongue along the top row of her teeth. Why hadn't she put a little lipstick on to brighten herself up? She was as pale as a ghost: her reflection shocked her in the café's mirror. She ordered a coffee and a Danish pastry. The woman said 'Here you are, dear,' and seemed to relate to Irene as if Irene was normal so that was something. That was surely something.

There hadn't been a word of warning. They had not been getting on as well as in the early days, but all marriages descended into squabbles and squawks and shrieks and silences. In the early days, Irene could no wrong and in the late days Irene could do no right. That was the journey of their marriage from right to wrong. Iain criticized just about everything. He even said Stupid Woman fairly regularly. Irene disliked Iain doing his crossword puzzles. When they were first married she was proud of his smartness. Working class, scholarship boy, went to Allan Glens. But as time went on his cleverness seemed so self-contained, almost exclusive. Irene couldn't get in. It was all double Dutch to her: crossword puzzles. It seemed as if Iain was often cross doing them or correcting them the next day. 'Christ. That was staring me in the face,' he'd shout at the obvious answer.

But it had come from nowhere. One evening at dinner when Mary Ann was out, Iain had said simply and coldly, 'I just can't do it anymore.'

'Do what dear?' Irene said.

'This. This bloody marriage. It's a farce. We don't even love each other. The sex is practically non-existent and not very good. I'm packing my things.'

It was typical of Iain that even as he was leaving he had to blame Irene. All her fault like everything else. She was the inadequate one. No, 'Sorry.' No, 'I'm in love with someone else.' No tears. Just a tight cold stranger's face.

She took a knife, a fork and a spoon and a napkin from the café when the kind woman wasn't looking. She put them in her raincoat pocket. She went to the pond where the Canada geese and the moorhens and the white geese and the male and the female mandarins lived out their theatre on the water, remembering and forgetting their lines. She took the bread from her pocket and fed the birds. They knew her. She knew them.

She peered in and saw her reflection wobble and distort. The wind forked her hair. Kneeling, almost crawling, she set an empty place for herself at the side of the water. She put the knife very carefully on the right. The fork on the left. The spoon at the top. Then she sat back spreadeagled on the grass, both legs sticking out in opposite directions, like a child. At her place, Irene methodically cut her way through bits of grass and turf. Her mouth was full of the taste of earth, iron. She wiped the side of her mouth with her napkin and continued chipping and chiselling and chewing. There was nothing like it. A picnic to herself at the park with the Canada geese watching Irene and Irene watching the Canada geese.

Wha's like us

The oldest woman in Scotland

The oldest woman in Scotland still bakes. The day she stops baking she will stop being the oldest woman in Scotland. She bakes although none of the other people living in her sheltered housing scheme, The Rowans, ever has her round to their house. But they always come to her house. Ring the bell and shout, 'Are you in? Are you in?' knowing full well she is never out. Knowing that all her groceries are bought for her by her youngest daughter, Elsie, who is seventy-two. Oh they all come and fair gobble up her baking. Her light sponge, her moist fruit loaf, her treacle scones. Into their old crumbling mouths, the crumbling cake goes. Some of them have not the wherewithal to wipe their old mouths and are quite capable of sitting there with crumbs stuck to their chin and a milk moustache for the whole length of an afternoon. Just as the old swines are perfectly at ease sitting about her place, until the oldest woman in Scotland has to boot them out. To do that, she has to stand up and go to the door. For they won't take a hint. She has to stand up, go to the door, yank it open and say, 'Is it not about time you were home?' Oh the old articles can't take anything subtle.

No one will ever think of taking his or her plate through to the kitchen to help the oldest woman in Scotland even though she is the oldest woman in Scotland. Nor of giving the plates a wee wipe. She has to stand by the sink, at her age, a hundred and six, and rinse them under the cold tap. She has never had a lazy day, or a long lie, in her life. The idea of having a long lie upsets her. What would anybody want with lazing around, stinking in their pits whilst the sun just goes up and up and up? How could anyone bear to lie about in old bedclothes, reeking and sweating and snoring on a fresh, clean morning? It is strange to her this idea of the long lie. Do they dream more vivid dreams when they have these long lies? It makes her dizzy to contemplate it. She cannae understand it. And of course it hides pure idleness. The long lie is designed for people who were brought up ignorant of the meaning of hard work.

The reason the oldest woman in Scotland is the oldest woman in Scotland is down to hard work. Give hard work its due. If it hadn't been for the fact that as a young woman she walked all the way from Lochgelly to Alloa to thon sheep dye place and then all the way back – three hours walking a day, never mind the work and the awful dye on her fingers; if it hadn't been for the washing the back of seven miners and their moleskins – and this in the days before the washing machine, think about it; if it hadn't been for the constant nose to the grindstone of the sewing, the cooking, the cleaning, the oldest woman in Scotland would not be alive today. And although modest to the end of her hemstitch on her long narrow skirt, she will admit that for her age she is looking good. Better than some of them that are twenty, even thirty, years younger. True enough: the fine blush that used to appear on her cheeks willingly now has to be coaxed on with a bit of rouge. The real colour went when she become one hundred, the same year that she gave up her pipe at night. The eyes are drooping and dropping and dark now, there's no denying it. And the sparkle has gone. She's dull to herself when she looks in the mirror. And the teeth are not her own, have not been her own for years now; so long, in fact, that if real teeth were to suddenly smile in her mouth, she'd be alarmed, frightened. She'd think they might bite. There's a comfort in these odd flat false teeth. The way she can move them around, the clucking sound she makes as she does so, if she wants another noise in her house; the way she can just get rid of them altogether at night and watch them float like wee sharks in the glass beside her. You couldn't do that with the real ones. You couldn't just yank them out when they annoyed you. But her hair is all there and not as thin as Agatha Anderson's or as cheap-dyed-looking as Nan Fraser's or as old-woman-looking as Helen Macintosh's. Yesterday, the oldest woman noticed that not only is Agatha Anderson's hair thinning, but bald patches gleam like atrocious secrets underneath the straggly hairs. Poor Agatha. And her only in her early eighties too. A youngster compared with the oldest woman in Scotland. A skittery jittery youngster.

But look at her hair. She's got to admit that her hair does not look like the hair of a woman who is one hundred and six years old. It is pure white, where it used to be blonde, but it is still thickish and has a bit of a bounce in it. The girl comes to the house on a Wednesday and does it for her.

'Massage deep!' The oldest will command in the middle of her shampoo. 'Harder!' If you work hard all your life, your scalp will respond. Your scalp will not give in to dandruff or alopecia or a dry, damaged demeanour. If you work hard and look after yourself and eat the right foods, you'll keep your hair; you'll not end up being one of those bald, hard-faced Scottish women that go about the place buying bargains. For years she's known this secret to health. Hard work. Aye. There's many that will shirk from hard work, including ones in her own family. But she's no shirker. The shirkers always fall down with mysterious illnesses, the like of which she has never heard. Diseases, she's quite sure, the lazy folk have gone about the place inventing.

The oldest woman in Scotland has had the flu four times in her life. Piles after she gave birth – like big black sour plums. A bit of arthritis in her hips, but not thank God, her hands. Mild angina pains. Now that she is cracking on, spanned two centuries and a new millennium, lived to see the new Scottish parliament, to see everybody go mad with computers and mobile phones, to hear everybody talking about sex, the oldest woman in Scotland would like to see the basics acknowledged: hard work, very little alcohol, no long lies.

In her day you were never told anything about sex. Not a word. The words they use these days, the oldest woman in Scotland scandalizes herself, oh God's trousers! The words they use. The things they do. She never knew anything about any of it. You just lay there in the dark mostly. When Edward the eighth abdicated, the oldest woman in Scotland was in bed with her husband, when she had what she now realizes was her first and only orgasm. It shook her about like the only shortbread in a tin. A great big wha-hay inside her. The man's clipped voice on the wireless going on behind her: 'I can no longer perform my duties without the help and support of the woman I love.' That was what, 1936? It never happened again, that wha-hay.

Outside the house of number eight The Rowans is a blue plaque which reads: *Herein lives the oldest woman in Scotland.* It worries her what will happen to this plaque when she goes. Will they give it to the next oldest woman in Scotland – who is bound to be younger than her by a mile? Bound to be a bit of a cheat. (One of they yins that has hidden her birth certificate and is actually pretending to be older than she is to get the benefits.) Or will they change the wording and put *Herein lived* – of course she'd have a preference for the second choice if anyone were to consult her. Chance would be a fine thing.

This morning she is up at her usual time, seven o'clock. It is her birthday. She is one hundred and seven. Another year in, she says to herself and shakes her head back and forth, a bit of a wobbly shake. Well, there's one thing for certain: the oldest woman in Scotland is not getting any younger. What kind of day is it? It takes her a while to pull back the curtains: she has to move them along bit by bit by bit. A good five minutes. Once, she would have given them a sharp tug and the sky would have suddenly appeared. How many days is that now that she has seen the sky? What would it be like to open the door and there be no sky? No swirling, rushing clouds. No flame reds and oranges, no dusky pinks. No great big blue up there, always there, always seeing. Half the time the sky looks like she feels, weary and wabbit. It is drizzly, wouldn't you just know it, dreich, and not a day for going out. Yet out she must go today. For her daughter is holding a little party for her. She shuffles into her bathroom and washes her face with cold water. (The secret to her good skin.) She gets herself dressed which takes a tedious amount of time. Pulling on her drawers, her tights, her vests, her blouse. The buttons are nigh near impossible now. They slip out of her soft thumbs and she's got to try again and again to manage the blighters. Today she'll wear her purple cardigan; people have admired her in that. And some pearls round her neck. A dab of rouge and a swipe of lipstick. She's vain still and she knows she is vain. She pushes her feet into her navy blue shoes. Lovely leather with a bit of a heel. If only she'd been born just a couple of inches taller. Not a lot to ask. A couple of inches.

She's not feeling like going out today. She hardly goes out at all now, and when she does the bite and snarl of the air just about knocks her for six. It fairly barks in your face, the wind, like a bad-tempered auld dog. She pulls her scarf on, ties a firm knot under her chin with difficulty. Her neck is wrinkled now. Wave after wave of wrinkled skin as if she was more complicated now, folded into one silence after another. She's all ready for the granddaughter, come up from England for the occasion with her English-speaking son and daughter, to collect her in that snazzy silvery blue car.

The oldest woman in Scotland's daughter does not bake, though she was well taught. Hold the sieve high in the air. Crumble the butter and flour between your fingers till you feel it change. Beat and beat till the top of your arm hurts. 'Does it hurt? No? Well, you're no done yet.' Today, on the oldest one's one-hundred-and-seventh birthday, she knows she must face a shop-bought cake with too hard icing; and she knows that she must try and find it within herself to smile.

'Smile, Great-Gran! Say cheese' shouts her youngest great-grandchild in that grating English voice. She smiles, a wee thin smile sliding along her lips, not letting her teeth show. She doesn't like toothy smiles or grins that make her appear goofy. At one hundred, she'd said to them, 'Right that is the last photie o' me ever to be taken.' But would they listen. The granddaughter even had the nerve to call it 'documenting a phenomenon' to which the oldest one had said, 'Pshaw.' But privately thought that maybe she had a point. Right enough. There's no many. When you get this high up the ladder. This far up the mountain. And you look down and see the whole human race scurrying to be where you are. And you watch so many drop like lemmings. So here she was with her dignity wrecked again, leaving another daft picture for posterity, sitting on that sofa with her son-in-law, daughter, grandchildren and great-grand-children, smiling like some daft old loony. 'Come on, great-gran, you can do better than that! Everybody shout sizzling sausages!' In the name of God. 'Sizzling sausages!' they all shout loud enough to break the inner drum of the oldest woman in Scotland's ear.

The table is laid with bits and pieces and everybody's tried, true enough. But there's no home baking. And the tablecloth is paper! Paper with big flowers painted on it. 'Do you like my table?' her youngest daughter says, exchanging a look with her granddaughter. They are a right pair those two for exchanging looks and shrugs and raised eyebrows and they think she doesn't see them. 'Flower of Scotland, isn't it bonny?' Her son-in-law bursts into loud singing. He's given to doing this, her son-in-law, bursting into song whenever she comes as if he has to sing to get through it. As if he just cannae stand to talk to her. 'Oh Flower of Scotland, when will we see your like again,' his mouth full of food. 'That fought and died for your wee bit hill and glen . . .'

Crumbs spray out of his mouth like tiny sprigs of heather. Elsie is that dignified, Elsie has got decorum. But no him. It still sticks in the gullet although he is seventy-six, too old to change and she is one hundred and seven, and doesn't need to change.

She notices he is the only one that has not bought her a wee gift. 'Open your presents Great-Gran,' they are all shouting. So she opens them. Chocolates. She'll have two of them a night with the telly till they are all done. A new nightie. What's she wanting with nighties, she's got plenty. A new cardigan. What's she wanting with cardies, she's got plenty. Bubble bath. Her bathroom's choking with bath things. She could live to one hundred and thirty and still be clean and smelling wonderful – no need to spend on soap or bubble bath or bath salts or bath cream or sponges or flannels or scrubbing brushes until the day she dies. A bottle of Grand Marnier. Well. She'll take a wee nip of that when the nights are drawing in. Warm the old blood.

The daughter is out of breath from all the effort of the wee party, as if it had been hard work when it is all shop-bought. 'Are you all right, Mum?' she says, waiting for the oldest woman in Scotland to pay her a compliment. Well, she will not be forced into compliments. She's too old to be false. 'Aye, fine, fine,' she says and sups the tea that is far too weak. Suddenly someone shouts for speeches and her great-grandson stands up on a chair and says: 'We are gathered here today to celebrate the birthday of our great-grandmother who also happens to be the oldest woman in Scotland. We wish her health and we are proud to have her in our family. Each year she gets a card from the Queen, but the Queen doesn't love her like we do.' The speech moves the oldest and a few tears come out the corner of her eyes. It would have been perfect if only the great-grandson didn't have an English accent like Edward the eighth. She had to keep saying to her daughter, 'What's that he's saying?' and it just about spoilt it for her. An awful shame when families move away to England and lose their good Scottish tongues. The young boy doesn't even ken who Rabbie Burns was.

They look a queer family anyway, all lined up on the couch for the camera. There's her youngest, her favourite daughter, Elsie, who has still got braw skin like her mother used to, a natural bloom in her cheeks; there's her scruffy son-in-law, no even able to put on a proper shirt for the occasion, his hair falling in every direction; there's her overweight black granddaughter with her bonny face and her dark eyes, her long dangling earrings and her big bosom; there's the great-grandson, black as the Earl of Hell's waistcoat, with such tight, tight curls on his head and his eenty teenty English voice; and there's the great-granddaughter with her long loose black curly hair and her cheeky wee smile. All lined up on the couch, putting on their faces.

A home help that came to the oldest woman in Scotland's sheltered house once said, 'Ooooh, who's that you're with?' And the oldest woman replied, 'My grandchildren and great-grandchildren,' The nippy girl said to her, 'How did that happen?'

'How did what happen?' the oldest woman in Scotland practically shouted at the home help.

'Well, they're black and yet your daughter and her husband are white, but tell me to mind my business!' she said, holding her duster in the air.

'My daughter adopted them,' the oldest woman in Scotland said, trying for the right note in her voice.

'Well, that was brave,' the home help said and busied herself with the dusting.

'They've got braw skin like mine,' the oldest woman said, sensing an insult somewhere.

As she gets older, the insults become more sneaky and clever and she has to be on her toes, sharp as a tack to pick them up. People think just because she's old they can get anything past her. 'Why don't we open your chocolates now, Great-Gran?' the English boy pipes up. The oldest one gives him a sharp look then starts to pull at the cellophane. No sooner have they given you something than they're taking it back. She watches him pluck two from the dark box.

'Can I have one of my birthday chocolates?' she says in her hard, hard-done-to voice. Her daughter does the strange breathing again. 'What's the matter with you?' the oldest woman in Scotland swings round and faces her daughter. 'You're all red in the face.'

'Don't start, Mum,' Elsie says, pleading as if she was just a young lassie. Oh if she could just take a swipe at her, a good hard swipe across her face. 'Give him the chocolates,' the birthday girl shouts. 'Give him them! Let him eat the whole box. I don't care.'

'Don't be so silly. Don't spoil your birthday,' says Elsie.

'Here,' the oldest woman says, grabbing on to her great-grandson's arm, 'Here,' she says, pushing the big box of chocolates into him. 'Have them.'

'Thanks.' Would you believe it, that's what the wee blighter says, 'Thanks' and goes off to scoff her birthday chocolates.

Her granddaughter intervenes. 'You can't go off

with your great-gran's birthday chocolates,' she says and goes to take them off him. He resists and the whole box spills on the floor. 'Oh for goodness sake!' her granddaughter says.

'You see!' the oldest woman says moving forward in her chair to look at the sight of her birthday chocolates all over Elsie's carpet. Pure greed. 'I never even saw a chocolate when I was a wee girl,' she says to her great-grandson. 'Never even set eyes on one. A banana was a big treat.'

'A banana!' he laughs.

'You kin laugh,' she says.

'Who would have believed it, one hundred and seven!' the son-in law says with some weariness. 'What a woman!'

Strange though, how the older she gets, the younger she sees herself in her own head. Memory is a strange bugger. Her life keeps stripping itself back to when she was a girl. Oh she can see herself so vividly. Now that she's this old, everyone is after her for her memories as if they were valuable, as if they were worth something. They come and they want her to talk into tape recorders so that she can be a living record. Nobody was ever interested in a single thought she had when she was sixty-seven, seventy-seven, eighty-seven. It was only when she reached ninety-five that the memory sharks really descended. 'I've seen times,' she'd say. 'Oh I've lived through some times.' And all the time, the picture of herself with her thick blonde plaits and her green dress would fill with colour. When you get this old, you start to go back, she'd say. 'You start to return.'

'What are you thinking Great-Gran?' her wee granddaughter asks.

'I've not seen Ethel or Agnes or Billy or Andrew or Iain and at that funeral they didn't so much as acknowledge me and . . .'

'Mum!' says Elsie. 'It's all in the past. Forget it.' The daughter does the strange breathy breathing again.

'That family of mine,' the oldest woman in Scotland continues as if she had not been interrupted, 'That family of mine will send me to an early grave.'

'An early grave?' her daughter says. 'An early grave?'

A guid Scots death

Ken this: you're born; you live; you die. It comes doon to this. The cost of ferrying you from hospital to parlour to crematorium. Forget the future. Forget it. You're no making it to next year. Your skin is hinging off. All this talk aboot time all the time. I've had it up tae here.

I'm trying to remember what I was told about my own birth. Ten a hauf pounds. Midnight. My maw screaming for God. It doesnie mean onything. Even your own life, it turns oot, doesnie mean dickie bird. Your ain habits and likes and dislikes. Puff! and away they go. A wee show of stars and then the big, biding dark. Looking back tae this and furward tae that. It's no real so it's no.

I'll tell you what's real. Dying. I feel mysell relishing it. Folk are listening tae what I'm saying like my words are gold. Hinging on my every pronouncement. I cannae shout ma words anymair. Thur whispered oot. My voice is dimmin doon noo. So they're leaning, sinking, faces close, close. They could be inside me. I'm this close tae them. My own death – this close. Right up agin them. Close as a breath intae the oxygen mask and back again roon my own chin. I'll no be forgotten. I will be forgotten. No, I'll no be forgotten.

I'll no see my Japanese jugs ever again. Or my wee sheltered hoose. But by Christ, I've lived a life and a hauf; I've made it tae my age, wi' all my bits and my ain hips and nae plastic in me at all. And that's mair than I can say for some folk a lot younger! But I'm no looking as young as I could because I lost my teeth. I don't know where I put them. They're either in my hoose or in the ambulance. I dinny like people to see my gums. It looks that ill tae see, an auld woman wi' a sunk chin, dribbling.

Here I um. I've got an oxygen mask on my face that puts me in mind o' my rain hats. Pulled the string tight under my chin tae keep my hair nice. What a sicht in the rain. Oxygen masks on ma heid and bright red lipstick.

I'm running doon the High Street wi' a wean in each haund and I'm full of violence. My ain violence is snatching my breath. I stop and tug Pearl's brown coat, back and forth. She's girnie and crabbit and she's at it and she knows it. I've had it. I skelps her right oot in the street. None of this namby pamby, 'Whit do you think?' stuff that's making a mess of today's children. It's a guy dreich day and oor Pearl's hair is soaking wet and the rain is pouring doon my face and I cannae tell if it's the rain or tears pouring doon Pearl's. Bruce is smiling a sly smile that maddens me so I cuff him across his heid and tell him he's next. And he hings, lanky aroon the lamp-post, heid doon, scowling. And here the two of them are at my bedside. And I don't know if they're crying fir the past or crying fir me.

I've always had my opinions. There's folk that are empty-heided and when you ask them whit they think aboot such and such, they look glaikit and say, 'I'm no sure.' Nae fibre in them. Nae *All Bran*. Noo that I'm sitting right next to the big High Heid yin himsell, Mister Death, I find I've still got things tae say. Things I want said. I'm no feart aboot going. When I go, a lot goes with me. I know that because my kind are no made anymore. Everyone's that saft and full of excuses noo. Nae backbone.

I've always been a fussy wuman. Just like the wee robin that comes tae visit my sheltered hoose. The robin is an affy fussy bird. Same spot, same bit of the wall, every year. I'd gie it a bit o' the fat from my ham, it wouldnie take bread. My granddaughter brought some lavender oil and put it on my flannel; I had tae tell her tae get it aff. It was sickly sweet, an awful hippy smell like yon patchouli they flower folk used tae wear wi' their long hair. Nearly made me boke. I dinny like sweetness. I cannae trust sweetness. Whit is there to be sweet aboot? I dinny like a sweet smile, all sugary. I like a good soor smile. A smile that says, 'I kin still manage a wee smile despite all the horrific things that have been happening to me.' I like plain. I like soor. Gie me a soor ploom, a bitter lemon or a squeezed lime straight on to my tongue. Gie me a man wi' a long soor face so I ken where I um. I dinny like they men that trick you into thinking you could be happy, the ones wi' pressed sharp trousers and shiny shoes, dancing with long slow smiles.

My hands are all wired up noo. God knows what all is going intae me. Stuff fir my heart, my liver, my blood pressure. Drips tae stap me dehydrating. My haunds are covered in bruises all over. I dinny ken whaur they're going tae find tae put any mair needles in. I'm like the bionic woman there's that many wires in me. My hands have never shirked. I dinny even haud back from the needle.

I was work; work was me. I couldnie stop. Your whole body felt the work in you, nagging and goading your veins. I was fit. My airms had muscles like a big muckle man's. My back would be that sair from the hard work. Making yir fist tight, bloodless, scrubbing and rubbing hard. Right doon on your bare knees. It was like fighting – work. Yir anger came oot in ragged breaths till you'd rubbed it up guid. Roon an roon an roon an roon an roon. Pit a shine on it. Made it shriek wi' cleanliness. My elbows were working elbows, dry skin on them. My sleeves always rolled up for my bucket so they didnae get wet. Whit was a cut or a scrape tae me? By Christ, they don't ken work now. They don't ken by heid and horn that feeling in your body when yir body has been taen over, when yir body belangs tae work. But then I came hame, stane-tired and wabbit and they hudnie done whit I asked them to do. The dishes werenie touched. The floor wisnae swept. They'd feel it then, the back o' my haund.

And here they are at my bedside, Pearl and Bruce, the baith of them wi' too much beef on them.

Bruce wi' his baw face and wan o' they beer bellies. Pearl's still got a bonny face but her smile is a fossil through whirls and rolls o' fat. And here's me: never put on an extra pound in my puff. Never wasted a single meal. Here's me – skin and bone. My haunds all papery and wistful hauding my children's thick, big fingers. You dinny get used tae yir child's haund getting big. It feels wrang forever. I'd say tae them, when they were wee, gie me yir haundie and I liked the feeling o' it, the wee, innocent han' in my ain. Weel. Thur no innocent noo. Sometimes, I have tae pull my haund away because I still cannae staund to be touched for too lang. All my wurds have run oot and are dribbling doon my chin.

There's been plenty folk to see me. Lovely flowers. Cards. Folk leaving, greetin'. I can manage a wave wi' my wired hand like an old puppet. One of the men from The Rowans gave me a hug, leaning right over the hospital bed. I says, 'That's the first grope fray a man in seventeen years.'

We never talked aboot sex. No the way they do today. Oh my God. We didnae have the words for hauf o' what went on. We just did it in the dark. Lights oot and then the fierce fumbling. Wance, I gave oot a long slow moan, like bagpipes fillin' wi air – nyuuuuuuuuuuuuuuuur – fir I was quite enjoying it and my man sat bolt upright, snapped the light on, and cries, 'Whit's wrang wi' you?' He thocht I wis having a heart attack. That wis aboot the last time I had sex. I was nearly sixty. I didnae miss it that much. No that I can remember noo.

I've left my hoose neat. My pants are all folded

in my drawers. My blouses are all thegither in the wardrobe. My nighties are all clean. I've got fifty skirts she'll hae to give to charity. I've got plenty towels and flannels and god knows all what. I've aye been neat. I wis even a neat walker. I wisnae wan o' they clumsy wuman, ill-hung-thegither, gangly and ungainly, getting in everybody's way. I've got sma' feet. My feet have always been nice. Nice toes, the lot. Thur no coming apart wi' corns and bunions and dry skin. My bones are coming through now. My working bones. There's no going to be bones like this in the future. By Christ, no.

There's no a thing wrang wi' me except the auld heart's packed in. But them years younger have got illnesses I've never heard of. I think they make the names up. Jist the other day I wis hearing people noo believe men kin get post-natal depression. Well tae hell wi' that. People sad aboot the rain and the winter. People eating hail packets o' chocolate biscuits jist tae throw them up again. Folk that cannae eat a raspberry wi'oot their tongue swelling oot and throttling them. Royals having thur jobbies irrigated. Folk wi multiple personalities when one's enough. People wi M.E. Me me me. They're welcome tae it. I'm gled I'm jumping ship. Nae plastic hip fir me. Nae pacemaker. No walking stick. No blood pressure pills. No hearing aid.

I'd rather have somebody shout straight into my lug than wear a hearing aid. They don't look nice. They look like they could be alive, they strange pink things, like foetus in folks' ears. There's them that embrace the stick and the zimmer, that cannae wait tae get auld and stoop their back and moan and complain and curry favours.

The wan thing I conceded to wis false teeth. I couldnie o' managed wi'oot them. And noo I'm up a closie where I cannae find ma teeth. And I've no looked so auld in my life. I dinny want tae die wi'oot my teeth. I've had my daughter hunt my hoose for my teeth, bit nae teeth, nae teeth. Whit does it mean dying like this wi'oot your teeth? Wull it bring me bad luck. We used tae say if a bairn wis born with teeth, it was dreidfae unlucky. That bairn could grow up tae be a murderer. Auld wives' tales. Where will the auld wives go noo?

Auld wives like me. They'll drop the auld wives and the tales. And whit will they be left with? Sleaze and violence. The wurld is upside doon. It doesnie make any sense. There's no one to say dinny. Dinny, naw, because how else are the weans tae learn? The bairns today are indulged; their parents are feart o' them. It used to be the ither way aroon. But naw! Now the slightest whine and it's a poke o' sweets. Parents have tae bribe their kids tae get them to put on their claes. Oh Jesus. They are welcome tae it. The hale wurld is spinning oot o' control. The earth's boiling; you cannae eat the beef; there's folk still starving. But the fat sow's arse is always greased.

The auld wives are leaving time. Their long skirts and long faces that stood at the gate and watched whilst their man wis brought hame drunk on the back o' a coal cart. The auld wives that gossiped and blethered to create a toon. The wans that knew the men wuid let them doon. The men wuid drink the blood of the family. The blood wis drained from the auld wives' cheeks; the auld wives were peely-wally. And there wis the man, his cheeks a ruddy red, blood enough for all of them.

It's the auld wives lowsin time. The wans that never cried or foutered, scuttered or shied away from the truth. The auld wives that waved at the fishing boats and put on a brave face. The bonnie fechters, the wabsters weaving, plashing and plaiting. The auld wives that made sure a fresh loaf was brought intae the hoose in the new year. The wans that kept their bread bins clean for their mother-in-laws. The auld wives that never threw ashes oot on New Year's Day, feart o' throwing ashes in thur saviour's face. The auld wives that lit and blew oot the candles. The thrifty auld wives, the mourning auld wives, the credulous auld wives. The fish wives, the biddies, the weedows, the guid wives, the hens that rabbit on, all of them will be gone, gone. The auld wives that opened the doors tae let the auld year oot. They are going; they are going at Hogmanay. The wans wi' the grim, worked faces, the scarves over their heids. The wifies singing the auld songs since auld lang syne. *How can ye bloom sae fresh and fair? How can ye chant, ye little birds, And I sae weary fu' o care*. The loops and the looms and the landscapes lost, the banks and braes, the singers, the songs, the poems by heart, going, going. The auld wives are going awa', airm in airm away from the future.

Alang the ward, the char lady comes with a cup of tea I cannae drink. I dinny want food noo. I dinny want onything. All I want is a cold hand on my forehead, a cold flannel pressed into my skull. I want Pearl to pit water on her fingers and rub my tongue. All day lang, the nurses walk up and doon the corridors in thur uniforms.

This wire going intae my airm is thinning my blood. This wan is diamorphine. It will kill me in the end. This one is regulating my kidneys. This wan is taking oot ma urine. I'll never sit on a toilet seat again. The nurses are doing that much fir me. They are never away from me. All my wires, my drips, my bruises.

My oxygen mask keeps falling doon my face. The elastic at that back o' my heid isnae tight enough. But these young nurses will never become auld wives. Wance you've had the auld roond once, they don't come the same again. Neither do the weans. These young nurses have got my life in their hands and they're gentle wi' it.

My sight still sees. But everything else is getting weaker and weaker. I feel I could just slowly fade away till nothing wis left o' me but my skin and bone, lying on the hospital sheets. Along the corridor, I can see them coming, Pearl and Bruce, their faces all strained. It's as if they are saying to me, they cannae take any mair o' it. Pearl's got a strange wee smile on her face the day. She sits doon at the side o' my bed and rustles in her handbag. And oot comes my teeth. 'Dunaaaa!' says she, wi' a flourish.

'In the name of God,' I says to Pearl, 'Whaur did you find them?'

'They were at the back of the drawer in your mahogany dresser behind all your purses,' she says.

I sit up and shout, 'nurse, nurse, it's a miracle. Pearl's found my teeth.' And the nurse comes. I try and fit the teeth intae my mooth. It takes me the longest time fir my gums are too dry fir teeth. 'Noo,' I say to the wee pretty nurse, 'whit dae you think of me? Dae I look glamorous? At least I'll no be all gums for my leaving.' I say and Pearl squeezes my wired haund and greets, 'Oh Mum!' And dabs at her een. She looks at me as if she's proud o' me dying like this. 'Did you no ken yir mother had so much panache?' I says winking at Pearl. Bruce greets as well, silent-like. Mind, he always wis a greetin-Teenie.

I pu my teeth oot o' my mouth and lie them at the side, on tap o' the hospital cabinet. I fancy thur smiling at me, they teeth of mine. Pearl pulls my rain hat back over my heid and all I can hear is the sound of my own breath, going in, oot, in, oot, in, oot. Ye ken, it sounds like the sea, me. I sound like the sea. Haaaaaaaaah. Haaaaaaah. Awa. Awa. Awa.

Shell

She wakes five minutes before her alarm goes off at seven o'clock, throwing her duvet right back so that it doesn't get in her way. Then she rocks, back and forth, back and forth, until she has gathered enough steam to rise. By the time her alarm goes off, with its urgent and panicky bleeps, Doreen is standing by it. Straightaway, she switches it off but the bleeps continue to play in her head, an alien noise that upsets her. Before she wakes her son, she has the first shower. She stands under the water with her eyes closed tight and her tongue hanging out. Turning around slowly, so that the water can get on to her back. She sways from side to side, letting her weight be carried first on one foot then the other. The water on her back is deeply pleasurable. Every drop seems to stay for a second before sliding off. Using her long brush, she scrubs at her arms and legs for some time. She throws a massive beach towel around herself and dries what bits she can reach. Let the rest drip. It has been a while since she reached her feet. She can see that her toenails need cutting, but getting down to them would be a massive effort; she'd have to set aside a whole afternoon.

She dresses slowly watching the clock all the time: seven-twenty. She puts on loose adjustable trousers and a large T-shirt. She walks slowly to her son's room and whispers hoarsely, 'Louis, time to get up, Louis time to have your shower.' He grunts and goes back to sleep. 'Louis,' she says louder, 'Come on.' Standing by the bed, she allows herself to give him quite a shake. 'Come on. Up. Up. Up,' she says.

Louis sits eating a big bowl of Coco Pops while she has a grated apple in a bowl with a spoon. She holds the bowl in her hand, very close to her mouth, as if she was extremely short-sighted, and eats from it, bending her head towards it. The apple is moist. Her eyes are small and bright and dark. Louis scowls at her, but says nothing. He doesn't speak much in the mornings. It is possible to imagine him as an old man already even though he is only fourteen. An old man, crabby and rot-gutted, silent with his newspaper and his strong tea and his rack of a cough. Tut-tut tutting.

'Have you seen my trainers?' he shouts at her in a mad rush, running up the stairs. 'What have you done with my PE kit?' She doesn't bother to answer anymore. It all goes on around her and she watches the swirl, the hiss and rush of it. She can't bring herself to get involved. Louis stamps down the stairs, bag on one shoulder, watch still in his hand, blazer half on, half off. 'Come on, Mum. You're going to make me late,' he says in a voice twanging with irritation, regarding his mother standing in the hall with her overcoat open. She is standing there doing some kind of neck exercises. 'I must have been lying in a draught last night,' she says picking up the keys from the table. They fall out of her fist and Louis bends to get them, beside himself now. 'Come on, Mum, you're so slow.' Doreen knows Louis imagines she does this sort of thing deliberately. 'If you got up earlier, we wouldn't have to rush,' she says grabbing the keys and trying to keep them in her hand. She walks slowly out of the house and opens the car door. Louis is already in his seat, doing his hair again in the passenger mirror. 'I need a haircut,' he tells her. 'It is starting to look stupid already.'

'Your hair is short enough. You've just had it cut.'

'Look at it. It looks like an Afro now,' Louis says.

Doreen ignores him. His hair is less than a quarter of an inch long; he has no conception of an Afro. Easing herself into the seat, she turns the ignition and the old Citroën Bamboo bursts into life. 'All the black boys have short hair,' he says. 'My mates get it cut every two weeks.'

'So you've got to be the same as everyone else?'

'Of course I've got to be the same as everyone else.'

'Well, I enjoy being different,' she says. He makes the sucking sound that he's been making ever since he went to secondary school.

In fact the old man thing had happened right away, from the minute he was born. It was true, she was wary of him even then. She looked into the glass cot and saw the eyes of a strange old man peering out at her. A complete and total stranger, nothing like what she had imagined.

When she looks back on her life when Louis was tiny, it makes her giddy to remember how her breasts fell down or were pulled down by Louis's greedy insistent little mouth. He was at her, day and night and she was on her own. There was no father to be seen for miles around. Just her and her baby, the light and the dark. The high-pitched noise of a new-born's scream and the low hushing waves of her sighs. Perhaps she had been mad, but she imagined a baby would be company.

It is difficult now for her to drive. She has adjusted the driver's seat so that it is at an angle, almost in the sleeping position. It is a mercy that Louis notices very little about her except when she is about to meet his friends. She drops him off on the road near his school. He will not be dropped at his school because he finds her car too embarrassing. He turns and waves. She feels a moment's impulsive love. She wipes a tear away with the back of her hand. The skin on her right hand is beginning to crack. How long, she wonders, will he wave for? Another six months, a year? Already he is changing into a teenager, walking a cool black boy walk, slapping gel on to his hair. A faint, alarming moustache round his top lip makes him look oddly ridiculous like a small man in a silent movie. She watches Louis round the corner towards the school. He doesn't look back again.

Doreen drives slowly up the Princess Road. Other impatient cars ride up her backside and flash their lights. Some people drive past, shoving their fingers up. One bright red Mondeo passes her at high speed and the passenger holds a sign out of the window. It reads ASSHOLE. She wonders if they have other signs. Perhaps they have an entire collection of obscene signs in their car and they decide on the spur of the moment who merits what sign. Just as well Louis is still not in the car. Her driving embarrasses him. He would like her to drive fast, slick, in a cool car. Not the ancient green Citroën Bamboo that she drives. Since she stopped going into the office, she's lacked the confidence to drive fast. Sometimes, it is difficult crossing the road. There never seems to be enough time. The green is always over too quickly. It is not possible to take big strides anymore. Small steps, one at a time, are all she can manage.

Yesterday it took nearly the whole day to go to the shops and back again. Doreen was walking towards Wilbraham Road to buy some fish for Louis. Fish once a week, she insisted, whether Louis liked it or not, for his bones. It was raining and the streets were wet and slippery. She found herself veering off the pavement and suddenly there she was in somebody's front garden walking on the borders. She pulled herself away, but it was the strangest thing. She had to turn around and let herself back out through the front gate that she had no memory of walking through in the first place. Closing the gate furtively, she glanced up at the house. Luckily nobody was there. The same thing happened a couple of minutes later, though that time she found herself bending right down sniffing, not even a rose, but the earth. When she finally made it to the fishmonger's, it was difficult to tell him what she wanted. She had to resort to pointing at a snapper and nodding her head.

Today Doreen passes most of the day in bed, sleeping. She has set her alarm for when Louis comes home just in case she doesn't wake. It is not like her to be indolent or lazy. Normally she is at it the whole time: washing, ironing, cleaning, cooking; never stops, never has a minute. Just recently, something has been happening to her body; her lower back is in agony and she feels heavy like a crate full of goods, lethargic and exhausted. A kind of tiredness she has never known. She could sleep from the late summer through to the end of winter were it not for Louis.

The alarm rings and she rolls over and bangs it off. It is difficult to get up now: she has to roll on to her side and then push herself up. Her whole back feels very unstable as if it could crack, as if her spine could slip and slide further and further down herself until it disappeared. A heap of crunchy, cracking, brittle bones on the floor. If her back cracked, a different Doreen altogether might come out from the inside. For the past couple of months, she can't escape this certain feeling of another woman living inside her, quietly. Briefly, she considers going to a doctor and then dismisses it. Doctors only make you worse, not better, she tells herself. The pain will go. Maybe it's been brought on by all that gardening, carrying alkaline bags of compost to plant camellias and azaleas. So stupid, stupid, stupid to heave those hefty bags of compost about the garden. The pain would pass; it would move on somewhere else, maybe to somebody else – though she'd wish it on nobody.

Eventually the pain would just go away, surely. Although, right now, sitting inside the pain, it was difficult for her to conceive or imagine anything else.

Louis comes in and dumps his bags down in the hall and goes to raid the cupboard. 'How was your day?' she asks him. Her voice is slow and thick, but Louis doesn't seem to notice. 'All right,' he says. Never gives much away. Never tells more than he has to. There was a time when she longed for details of teachers and lessons and friends and school dinners, but all that is in the past now. She lets him tell her what he wants; she doesn't plead for more.

On her back, she lies down on the living room floor. She puts two hard books under her head. One of the girls in her office told her about this. She bends her knees and puts her feet flat on the floor. Louis comes in with his cheese sandwich. 'You should have seen me today, Mum,' he starts. 'At football. I nutmegged him, then I kicked the ball like this.' (She follows the fancy footwork while lying on the floor. She can see just his feet out of the corner of her eye.) For some reason, Louis has decided to talk at her though the idea that she might have anything to say hasn't crossed his mind. No, he simply wants to show off. He does this occasionally, holds forth at some length on his various attributes and talents. Just her luck. Just when she longs for the usual silence, the dependable sulleness. 'Then, right, I did this amazing scissor kick like this,' his feet sweep across the small grey carpet, 'and I ran forwards, Michael passed it to me because I'd got myself in a good position, and I lobbed it and it went right into the back of the net.

Goalie didn't stand a chance. Why are you lying on the floor?'

She shuts her eyes for a minute, trying to press her bad back into the carpet. If she could just press the pain out of herself using her willpower. But she finds she hasn't got willpower anymore. She can't think straight. It is doubtful whether she will manage to fry Louis's fish. She'd meant to cook it yesterday but by the time she got round to it she had run out of energy. She sent Louis out for a Kentucky Tower Burger instead. Today she must cook the fish or the fish will go off. She drags herself up off the floor, knowing she has to make the effort, she has to fry the snapper and boil the rice and cook the hot tomato sauce. She lumbers into the kitchen and pulls the red fish out of the fridge with her fat fist. She can no longer stand straight. She is bent, like an old woman. The skin on her back feels as if it is stretching and straining, as if it wants to belong to another body. She doesn't blame it. The smell of the snapper is distasteful to her. Never again will she cook it, good for bones or not good for bones. It makes her want to vomit. She takes a cherry tomato and pops it into her mouth. The juice bursts alive on her tongue. It helps. Out of a bag of lettuce, she pulls a fistful of colourful leaves and presses them into her mouth. Her tongue feels quite hard.

When she has finished cooking Louis's dinner, she just about manages to carry the plate over to the table and put it down. It has been a dreadful effort and she needs to sleep. But she forces herself to sit down across from her son to keep him company. She eats some shredded cabbage from her bowl. Another thing: she likes now to eat from the same bowl every day and drink only water from the same cup. Her eyelids are heavy, she feels them droop; she feels the dreams crawl out like tiny insects and rest on her lids. She can't help herself; the neck gives in, shuddering a bit before it falls on to her chest. It looks broken; she could be praying. Her big neck lurches and crashes. Off she drifts sitting across from Louis at the table. It is some time before he notices. Maybe her breathing changes. 'You're not listening are you?' Louis says. His voice sounds irritated. 'What did you say?' she asks him, jerking awake, startled, frightened. 'It doesn't matter. Nothing,' he says. 'If you're not listening. What is the point in me speaking?' He makes that sucking noise again. 'No respect,' he says. For some reason these days, Louis is obsessed with respect. She doesn't even think he knows what the word means. 'I'm just so weary,' she says. She can tell Louis hasn't liked the word *weary.* He chucks it back at her: 'How come you're *weary* when you've done nothing all day?' he says. 'Exactly what I'm wondering myself,' she says watching his forehead as the fury sweeps across the high plain. 'Perhaps I need a lover,' she says. 'Maybe a lover would give me some energy.' She smiles to herself as Louis bangs out the room. 'Nobody would have you,' he shouts down the stairs.

Back to the floor, with the big atlas and a book of quotations underneath her head, she imagines what it would be like to have a lover. It has been a long time since she had one. The thought of somebody exploring her body, her rolls of fat, her big thighs, her fat dimpled arms, is exciting. Perhaps a new lover could come along and wake up her rolls of flesh. Maybe a tongue could lick under the folds. A lover could reach parts of herself she hasn't been able to find. It would be nice to have a woman lover, Doreen thinks. A big round soft woman like herself. With a big belly and big breasts. The two of them could roll and roll and fall right off the bed. The two of them could laugh into the dark. She shut up shop to men years ago. Just shut up shop. It was too earnest somehow for her, too humourless, all that shoving and pushing. All those smarmy, charming lies. She could trust a big fat woman not to lie to her.

Louis would not like her to have a woman lover; Louis wouldn't like her to have any lover at all. It would be almost worth going on the hunt for one just to see the look on Louis's face. But no, she is beyond love, really. She knows this. It is not for her, the bothering about what to wear, waiting for the phone to ring, the terrible silly beating of the heart.

Climbing up the stairs takes an age: she sways from side to side on the stairs, willing herself forward. By the time she gets to the top, it is nearly dusk. The house is cold; why is the house so freezing cold when it is supposed to be the summer? 'Turn the heating on full blast and finish your homework!' she shouts down to Louis. 'But it's not cold,' he shouts back, always liking to contradict, never able to follow a simple instruction. 'Just turn it on!' she bawls. 'I need heat. I'm not well.'

Louis appears at the bathroom door with his

homework. 'Mum, how shall I do this?' he says in that way he has that is both aggressive and demanding. 'I'm in the toilet for God's sake. Give me peace!' she shouts.

In the bathroom, Doreen sits for an age while a long, thick piss drains out of her. Hobbling around the toilet bowl, she looks down to see what's going on. Her piss is white and thick – the kind that birds do. There is something badly wrong with her. Maybe after a good night's sleep. Doreen decides to sleep in the boxroom where the bed is hard for her back. Under the covers, she digs, snuggling down deep, burrowing. She is cold. Her back is ice. She leaves the small bedside light on, just in case, turns on the electric blanket even though it is summer. The heat warms her thighs first.

When she wakes up the next morning her back is rock hard. She can just about feel it when she bends her elbow. Something is growing on her back. Her balance is totally affected now. She cannot stand still for a second; she sways from side to side to keep herself upright. The skin on the back of her left hand is cracking too. So too is the skin on the heels of her feet. Huge cracks seem to have taken place overnight. She tries to bend her leg to feel the ridges in her feet. They are really quite deep, the cracks. Her skin looks thick and yellow on the soles of her feet. The cracks are so definitive they could be part of some mosaic. The lines remind her of the bit of crazy paving she has out the back in her patio.

A part of her feels really curious, almost proud, about what is happening to her. It reminds her of how she always wanted a graze to look really bad when she was a girl, so that she could say, 'Look what happened to me.' Nothing nicer to show off than a bit of raw, red flesh. This back is like that. Part of her doesn't want the whole strange business to stop. Wherever it is she is going to, she is on the journey now; she doesn't want it to end; she doesn't want to get off, ever. All she wants to do is follow, keep going slowly further and further on, digging deeper and deeper till she might emerge from who knows where. Eventually, she might end up being a different person altogether, with a different life, another past entirely.

That night she cooks Louis chicken and rice and peas and watches him shovel it down. He eats everything. He is not fussy. She eats some raw chinese cabbage. She bends her head down and eats straight from her chosen bowl. Louis looks up and says, 'Are you not having any of this?' It has been some time since she has eaten any meat or anything cooked, but Louis hasn't noticed. 'No,' she says, 'You tuck in.' She watches Louis help himself to more from the pot, spilling some of the gravy on the floor.

'Clean it up,' she manages to say.

'Mum, I'll get it later,' Louis says, 'my dinner will get cold, Mum.'

She bends her neck close to the table and continues eating from her bowl. He says the word *Mum* much more often than he needs to. Constantly saying it Mum this and Mum that, drawing it out as if it was a long word. She wonders why he does that: perhaps he doesn't think she is his mother at all.

That night she runs herself a bath. Not a hot bath, a tepid bath. She can't wait to get into it, climbing and crashing straight into the water. Some of the water spills out of the bath with the impact. She looks down at the sodden floor, vaguely amused. Big bodies make big splashes. Doreen cannot lie back now; her back is too swollen, too large. Splashing the water up, she attempts to throw it round herself on to her back. When drops do reach there, the sensation is quite pleasurable. Moments pass slowly, peacefully, till she surprises herself by feeling something come out of her. The heat of the water has brought it against her will. She looks at her own turd floating in the water. This has never happened before either; it is quite curious, quite involving. A very long and thin, ribbony turd floating as if it had not a care in the world, like a canoe on a river. As if to keep it company, a piss arrives, too, with a hiss and a sigh. It is that thick white again. It reminds her of the time when she was a girl and she did a white motion in Wythenshawe Hospital. What a terrible shock that had given her until the nurse explained it was caused by the barium meal she had drunk for the X-ray.

The next morning she peers at herself in the mirror. She can't see herself all that clearly, but she can feel herself. If she tries to put her arm behind her back, she knows it is there. It is hard, although it could crack; it is protective, it is loyal and trustworthy; if she wants to she can hide her whole head inside the musky damp darkness, the forgiving darkness. Simply pull her neck back and hide underneath that capacious carapace.

It occurs to her to wonder why this is happening to her, why she has been picked for this experience. Doreen knows she has not been the mother of her dreams. Her voice has not comforted; it has grated. She has not liked her own soundtrack. She has heard it too many times a day, raised, or repetitive, going on and on and on. A voice she never thought she would hear from her own mouth. She has not soothed; she has irritated. Of course she has had the decency to feel guilt. Until she became a mother she never knew what guilt was really. Once you become a mother, you get to know guilt intimately.

Perhaps the sun might feel good, the summer sun. Doreen doesn't drive home after taking Louis to school, after waving her mother's wave, she keeps on driving out towards Jodrell Bank. Not for the night stars inside the building. No, she has come for the buttercups. She lies under a rhododendron bush wondering how she should approach things, what to do. Although it is a pain, and a discomfort and a downright nuisance, part of her really likes her shell. She almost feels tenderly towards it, as if her shell is a lover, a solid companion that knows and accepts all her faults. Nothing could surprise or shock her shell now.

Since she had it, the neighbours haven't bothered her. She has retreated. She has gone from being an outgoing bubbly kind of a woman to a shy, introverted one. Being shy is quite sexy. She enjoys holding herself in, taking things deliciously slowly. Her own company is quite fulfilling. At last, she has learnt to live in the moment, to let it be, let it hang and swing and rock in the air. A moment has a smell, a taste, a sound. A moment doesn't go back on its promises. A moment spills and fills with music, light, airy, elegant music, strings.

Next to the arboretum is a generous field of buttercups, such a bright and thrilling yellow. Like a field of sunshine on the ground. She remembers how she used to love to hold a buttercup under a friend's chin – the intimacy, the secret knowledge. 'Yes, you like butter, oh, you don't, oh you do. Wait. Oh, it keeps changing.' She bends down and eats the buttercups, one after another, even the stems. Some buttercups are really quite tasty. Some have a lot of yellow on them, really a lot of bold yellow. She moves slowly over the field next to Jodrell Bank having her fill. The old greed is still there, but now it is a pure *boterbloeme* greed. The pleasure she gets from these ample gold-cupped flowers is more intense than any she can remember. When she has finished she finds some shade and lies down to sleep. The alarm clock is with her; she places it at her side in the middle of the grass and sets it for half an hour before Louis will come home.

When it wakes her, she cannot remember having spent a more deeply pleasurable day. What a day, under the shade of the bush, having had such a meal. The pain is having to get up, having to do things. She sways to and fro until she manages to raise herself from the ground.

Louis coming home. Being there to remind him to do his homework, to tidy his room, to change out of his uniform, to clean his shoes. It hardly interests her now. She could weep. It was during a big weeping session that her shell suddenly appeared on her back. While checking Louis's geography homework, she noticed that he still pretended he lived with his father. He had to write an essay on what his family would do on a visit to a quarry. Louis wrote long, detailed sentences about his father and everything that he would do in this quarry. Very little about her. According to Louis, if she went to a quarry, she would spend the entire time in the toilets. So she asked him how come his father gets to go about the place with a site identification book and she is stuck in the toilet when he hasn't even lived with his father since he was two? 'Because my dad is cleverer than you,' he said. It was that single sentence that did it for her. 'You don't even correct my spelling,' Louis went on. Time and again, she told him he would only remember words if he looked them up in a dictionary himself. But he had something. The odd thing was that she'd started to forget how to spell certain words. Easy words like weekdays: she had trouble with spelling Saturday and Wednesday. 'You don't even have a job,' Louis continued. 'If you had a job, I'd be able to get a pair of decent trainers, and Sky.' For a minute she couldn't think what he meant. How could she be expected to give her son the sky? How could she get up there and rip a piece of blue from it and pull it down? She stood, back bent, imagining it for a second. Louis with a brilliant blue piece of sky in his rucksack. Louis opening his rucksack and a cloud floating out. 'See, look at the state of you. Just standing there grinning like a moron,' Louis said, disgusted. Her son standing there, scowling, a look of green poison on his face, a look of hatred, and at the same time, a hard-done-to expression, an it's-not-my-fault expression. He stood making things up as if she was a total imbecile, as if her brain was the size of a pea. 'Less of the lip, Louis,' she said angry then, angry for the first time in weeks. An enormous pain burst forth from the middle of her back and then a terrible tightening. Louis stood staring at her. 'What have you got to say?' she said. 'Nothing,' he said and went out of the room slamming the door. Her shoulders curled around themselves as she felt a hot, searing pain shoot out between her shoulder blades and another stab across her lower spine. A heavy weight spread across the huge sweep of her back. Sounds came out of her mouth, stranger sounds than those she'd made when she was in labour. Grunts. Deep hellish roars. Fiendish curses.

The sensation of falling right down under the ground, as if everything in her body was pulling her downwards. As if her noises were coming from the deepness of the earth, the blackness of the moist ground. She was sweating. Panting. Small little breaths. Ha ha hoo. Like the breathing exercises she'd been taught by the Jamaican midwife. She was horrified. But she was also amazed at herself. She staggered to the mirror and tried to see her back. She stood sideways. She got another mirror and held it behind her to be sure. It was highly domed like the roof of an ancient church. The lines were quite beautiful, delicate. Her back was an olive-grey colour. She could see herself as some small cobbled street in a medieval town. Or as an early map. The intricate patterns on her back forming light circles. Like a view of fields from the air. There would be no need to worry about what to wear anymore. She wondered what Louis would make of it the next morning. She'd be the belle of the ball with a shell.

The next morning she made Louis his breakfast, a cooked one for a change. 'Aw, Mum, thanks,' Louis said and put his arm around a bit of her. He didn't comment on her shell. Whether he noticed it and was being polite, or whether he hadn't yet noticed, she couldn't tell. When she looked at him, she could only see one bit at one time. A brown vivid eye for a split second. A black hair. A lace on his shoe that looked like a long worm. 'I won't be able to drive you to school anymore, you'll have to take the bus to school like you do on the way home.' she said slowly. 'You're old enough.' She saw his lip move up and down. But she couldn't see his expression. 'Why, Mum? Why not, Mum?'

So he hadn't noticed. Just like Louis not to notice a thing like that. 'I'm a bit encumbered,' she said, knowing Louis would have difficulty with that word. Doreen herself didn't have a clue how to spell it.

When Louis left for school, she got down on her knees and crawled to the garden. It was much easier on all fours, a huge relief. She felt herself shrink and shrink, she felt the scales grow on her forelimbs and around the side until she felt a crusty, marginal edge forming. It was a glorious feeling of relief, close to euphoria. It was as if she had been turned inside out. She felt fantastically good. The world from down here was full of small simple pleasures. Her sight was still sharp, but different. All she could see up close was the sharpness of a blade of grass, the impossible darkness of the earth. She dug down into the soil moving over small black hills, behind bushes, moving surprisingly quickly, till she found the shade she was looking for. She jumped on a pink, juicy translucent worm and ate it hastily. She sniffed the dark earth for a snail.

It must have been such a long time before she heard him. In the distance, she heard him shouting, 'Mum! Mum!' She felt herself being lifted up. She pushed her feet anxiously forwards and back to try and resist. She withdrew her head into her shell and folded her heavily scaled forelimbs. She heard him say, 'Mum, can I get a video from Blockbusters, Mum?'

The tortoise can feel human breath like a wind. A hot tropical breath blew under her shell and in towards her snake-like neck. The boy ran his fingers over the shell, round the marginals, in towards the costae, up and down the vertebrals. The boy put her down again. The tortoise rushed off towards the bushes, the earth, the shade, the possiblity of a cricket, a snail, a worm.

Out of hand

Rose McGuire Roberts holds her hands up to the light, turns them, this way and that. There are things hands can do happily; there are things hands instinctively disdain. Sometimes life gets out of hand. Rose with her long beautiful fingers, with her half-moon nails. Rose with her smooth, black, hands: dark lifeline, dark heartline, small lighter branches of children waving at the edge of her palm. Somebody counted six once when she was young, six children bending round the side of her hand. Thank God they didn't know what they were talking about. Fifty years ago, these were the hands that clapped then came to England. Willing.

Twenty-six years old they were then. In their prime with their nails filed and shining. No calcium spots. No loose skin. No dry skin. No wrinkles. Twenty-six-year-old hands. Dancing hands, talking hands, story hands, moving, working hands. On the go the whole time, rarely still, rarely silent. Twenty-six years old, they arrived, elegant, black, skilled, beautiful hands. Ready and willing. Ready was the left hand; willing the right. What a thing for a hand to get to do. What a way to lend a hand. They held on to the ship's cold silver rail full of their own sense of importance. She rubbed them together and told them to stop shaking. She gripped one on to the other to stop the trembling excitement. To stop her hands flapping like flighty birds. To contain herself. Her breathing was fast. Her chest tight with anticipation. England, England, England! Here she comes!

Fifty years ago hand over heart. Rose McGuire Roberts stepped off the *Windrush* with her dab hands. Many hands make light work.

Today is an off day. They just come up, days like this, and grab her from nowhere. She is propelled into her favourite chair to sit and think and go over and over things. The more she thinks, the more she sees. Her daughter rushes about, forgetting herself. Her grandchildren sit in front of computers all day long, pressing buttons and killing people. Pow! Gotcha! Bad! Snide! Her son is so concerned about money, he hardly sees her. He could lose quite a bit of money just sitting chatting to his mother and having dinner. When he does come, he gets out one of those mobile phones and spends quite a portion of the time swearing at the battery which is always running out. So that's family. Her husband, Fred, is dead. Dead and buried in the wrong country. That's life. They always talked, Fred and she, of going back; but somehow it stayed just talk. Lots of talk. But talk just the same. And a strange thing started to happen in these talks with Fred; it was like the pair of them were just imagining their country. The images became so vivid they were afraid to go back.

Their own country seemed part of their mind. What if they could never get there? What if it was a disappointment?

So she is just sitting in her favourite armchair, newly covered in a cream floral pattern. Let everybody rush, rush. Let them all think their rushing is important. Running, rushing feet. Let them run round London, up and down the escalators, in and out of the city like mad dogs. She sucks her lips and makes a sound that she is still teaching her twin granddaughters. They are quite good at it, you know. Surprising.

Fifty years in England and look at the change in her hands. They are still her hands; she can recognize them. Just. But they are wrinkled on the back of themselves and swollen between her knuckles. And one of them, the right one, the willing one, is giving her quite a bit of bother. She can't use it properly: hold a pen, or a duster, turn a knob or twist a bottle top, clean her glasses, whisk an egg. Actually if a person were to look only at her hands they would think that she was older than seventy-six. Her face looks years younger. Everybody says so. 'You don't look your age you know.'

'Don't I now?' she says. 'Well, I don't feel like any spring chicken.' She likes that expression 'spring chicken'.

'Oh yes,' they'll say, 'You don't look sixty-five if you are a day.' Like she should be pleased. What's the matter with looking seventy-six; what's the matter with looking eighty? What happens to spring chickens anyway? But she is pleased, a little. If she admits it. Pleased that her face is smooth without hardly a wrinkle.

Her hands are older than her face. It is almost as if they came into the world a good five years earlier than she did and were hanging around disembodied, picking things from trees and stroking smooth materials, snapping their fingers and sucking their thumbs until the rest of her came along and they found themselves attached. Perhaps they did have a life of their own for a while. The thought is a comfort. Because once they came to England they certainly had no life of their own! At all, at all, at all.

Rose McGuire Roberts came down those *Windrush* steps. She already felt memorable as she was doing so. Step by step and staring down into the waiting crowd. Tilbury didn't look like England. A dock is a dock. There were people waiting to greet the boat, waving, welcoming. It was quite something. The ones waiting and the ones coming off. The willing hands. It was June. She never forgets the date: 22 June 1948.

It takes her a week to find a room. She dumps her heavy suitcase down and lines the drawer with paper so she has somewhere clean for her clothes. The room is sad and unfriendly, like the landlady. But she is not yet discouraged. Things will pick up. She can make the room cheerful. Maybe she can make the landlady cheerful. Rose opens her door and Mrs Bleaney opens her door further down the stairs. Her head peeps out. (She was to see this nosy head peeping out many times in the next couple of years.) 'Going out are you?'

'I'm going to the cinema,' Rose says bubbling with excitement.

'The cinema, are you? Already? Don't be late back. I lock the door early.'

Rose McGuire Roberts sits herself down in the red seat. England, she is in England. She is in the cinema in England. How about that? Wait till she writes home to tell her mother. *I wasted no time! The day I found my lodgings, I went to the cinema! I used up a little of my savings for a big treat.*

Before *The Treasure of the Sierra Madre*, there is the Pathé news. And to Rose's absolute astonishment and disbelief, there she is up on the cinema screen on the news! It is herself right enough, coming off that ship. 'Last week in Tilbury, four hundred and ninety-four Jamaicans came ashore from the *Empire Windrush*. They have come to help the British economy. Many of them feel like they are coming home. Hundreds of people were gathered at Tilbury together. Welcome home. Welcome home.' Rose sees herself for a brief moment in black-and-white coming down the ship's steps with her red hat on. (Though only she knows it is red.) Her hat is tilted to the side and she is holding on to it. Her coat has blown open a bit and her smart navy dress is showing. She'd like to lean forward to the people in the seat in front of her and shout, 'That's me, that's me. That hat is red, that dress is navy. I know the colours she is wearing. She is me!' She watches herself come down the steps with the other people. For a moment, sitting there on her red seat, she feels the false shyness of a movie star. Didn't the person in front of her recognize her and turn round and stare? She'll have to watch out. At the end of *The Treasure of the Sierra Madre*, people might be asking her for her autograph! She practised it enough times before getting on the *Windrush*. People's handwriting in England will be very neat, she had thought to herself. Neat and elegant. English. English handwriting.

After the Pathé news, the movie begins. Rose leans forward in her seat. She has got a bag of sweets. She will wait till it is slap-bang in the middle of the movie before she opens them. In the dark cinema, she strains to see the time on her watch. All cosy, safe. *The movie was all about three losers searching for gold*, she imagines herself writing to her little sister back in Jamaica. *Humphrey Bogart was the star. Do you know who Humphrey Bogart is? 'They might get rich but they don't get lucky.'*

People start leaving the movie before the credits are finished. A lot of them stare at her as they leave. They definitely recognized her! No question! Only the stare is not friendly like you would expect. Well, maybe they are jealous! Maybe they wanted to be on the Pathé news! She sits and waits till every name has been and gone on the screen. When the credits finally finish, she is the only one left in the cinema. What an experience. Rose gets up and goes out into the tactless daylight. A little dizzy. It is a nasty shock after the cinema's chocolate darkness.

Rose McGuire Roberts can remember everything about those first few weeks in England in vivid colours. The red buses, red pillar boxes, red phone booths. The yellow-jacketed underground men. The green, green grass. When was it exactly that it started to change? After two weeks. Just two weeks?

She is a skilled nurse. Highly qualified. In Jamaica she was the youngest ward sister in the hospital. At Westminster Hospital, she is put on night shift. She stays on night shift for two years, even though she keeps trying to get taken off it. The night clings to her back; she can't escape it. Well, she never minded hard work. It's not the hard work that's the problem. It's the fact that she's been landed all the rubbish jobs, all the jobs she shouldn't be doing. Making tea, emptying rubbish, turning the patients in the night from left side to right side on her own, cleaning the bedpans. Somehow she ends up with all the bedpans to empty. How did that happen?

That was the beginning of it, Rose thinks to herself, looking at her hands. The back and the front. The right and the left. To think she had actually been excited by the idea of her hands coming to help, almost as if she could have sent them to England on their own. When she was young she never imagined that hands would age along with the rest of you and that it would upset her so. Well you don't imagine age at all when you are young. Look at her twin granddaughters now. When she tells them about herself as a girl, they think she is making it up! As far as the twins are concerned she has always been this old woman right here, right now. It is just impossible for them to picture her young with young hair, just as impossible as it was for her all those years ago to imagine herself old. She never thought she would ever look in the mirror and see this old woman looking back at herself. In her head she doesn't look like that. She can't quite believe how it all happened without her guessing it was coming. Just sort of sneaked up on her and then one day there was no more denying it. No, Rose, you are old.

All the bed pans in the world for her. Emptying the steel pans with the terrible crunched bits of hard tissue in them and the strong-smelling stools of the ill. Well, not so much stools as pouffes! Not even pouffes, pillows. Burst pillows! Explosions. That is it. English explosions. Night Shift at Westminster. Patients frightened. Shouting out, restless. They want their mothers even if they are old women and men. They fear death is coming to snatch them away. Sometimes death does come, right enough, in the dead of night with its long scratchy fingers. The white curtain gets pulled around the rail. The worried patient in the bed next door wakes to see the terrifying white curtain, quickly, quickly being pulled round the rail, the final curtain. The shuffling and whispering goes on and on. The terrible thudding movements. In the morning, just before Rose goes off her shift, the patients left behind stare the appalled stare of the patients left behind. The sight of that empty bed is too much for them. Once a woman shouts at Rose. 'You there! It's all your fault. You've brought your diseases with you. None of us would be in here if it weren't for you.'

What is so bad is not the nutcase of a woman shouting at her, but the fact that the other nurses are amused at her outburst. They shake their heads and smile helplessly. Not one of them says anything to help. Nobody intervenes. So the woman keeps it up. 'Keep away from me, keep her away from me.'

Rose would have liked to wash her hands of the whole country right then and there. Because nobody took the woman in hand. Nobody got high-handed with her and said, 'That's enough!' Rose McGuire's twenty-six-year old hands longed to slap the woman right across her face. To shout, 'Who do you think you are talking to!'

It wasn't just the one woman who was difficult. She was just the tip of the iceberg. She would never tell the twins about all that now. She doesn't want them to know. She didn't even tell her own children.

The next one, if she remembers right, was a man with a pinched face and a sharp irritable nose. Just as she was turning him over, he whispered hoarsely in her ear, 'Go back to the jungle.' She carried the sound of his fierce whisper all the way home. And home wasn't all that different because the landlady had a look on her face that said more or less the same thing. It got so bad that Rose could no longer tell which people had the look on their face and which didn't. It was difficult for her to trust anybody being nice. If somebody was pleasant, Rose would wonder why. She never used to wonder that. Never used to have this suspicion under her tongue, never used to suck on it like a poisonous sweet.

So what did she do? She went to the movies. She saved her money and went to the movies. Half the time she fell asleep in the cinema because of the night shift. She'd hear *The Secret Life of Walter Mitty* in the background and think dozily to herself, Is that him telling another lie again? *It's A Wonderful Life*, *The Red Shoes*, *Rope*, *Give my Regards to Broadway* in Technicolour, Bogart and Bacall in *Key Largo*, Rita Hayworth with her pretty auburn hair bleached in the gripping *The Lady from Shanghai*. 'It's true, I made a lot of mistakes,' Rita says in her dying breath. Rose watches Olivia de Havilland go crazy in *The Snake Pit*. Joan Fontaine in *Letter from an Unknown Woman*. Joan has beautiful hands. James Cagney in *White Heat*. 'Top of the world, Ma!' shrieks Cagney as he goes up in flames. Everybody is losing their mind, Rose thinks to herself, at home in the movies.

One day Rose McGuire Roberts stopped going to the movies. She came out of the cinema in 1958, a hot August day, to see Elizabeth Taylor and Paul Newman in *Cat on a Hot Tin Roof* with her husband in the year of the Nottingham riots. A group of white people gathered round the pair of them and shouted, 'Go back to your own country!'

This is the question she asks herself the most. How come she thought England was her country? How did that happen? How was it that she thought when she got on that *Windrush* that she was coming home?

It is late in the evening. The river is running slow. She closes the curtains. She washes her face and hands, then puts on some moisturizer. She rubs her hands in the cream, massaging it between her knuckles. She gets into bed. Even having a family didn't take away that lonely feeling. Because nobody knew. And her husband was a cheerful man. 'Don't dwell on it, Rose,' Fred would say. 'It'll eat you up.' But the thing about those off days is the more she dwells the better she feels. Oh no! Never tell people just to forget it. She has got to remember. She can see herself on a big screen. Red hat. Navy dress. Coming down off the *Windrush*. She could almost applaud. Was that some other girl? No. It was herself. Rose McGuire Roberts coming off that huge fiction of a ship.

Making a movie

Opening credits. My enemy makes movies. She is tall with a sharp nose. She's paranoid and thinks that everything is about her when everything isn't about her at all. I used to love her. She used to make me her own chapatis and this particular dish that I liked. I forget what it was now. It is a long time ago. It involved an aubergine. The time that she cooked it best she was wearing white jeans. I remember that like a flashback. Bringal bhaji. In her kitchen with white jeans on, waving a wooden spoon. It was impressive. The glorious ghee. That was it. I loved then to see unfamiliar things in a kitchen. The sight of fresh ginger, fresh coriander, long linked bulbs of garlic, I found exhilarating. I was impressed because I can't cook, not to speak of, not to remember. People who went to dinner at my enemy's house always spoke effusively about her food. 'Isn't she a good cook,' they'd say. Others in the know would nod greedily. It was an interesting house with a large conservatory at the back of it that her lover had built. Her lover was good with her hands. My enemy grew tomatoes there. I liked watching them turn from fairytale green to red. They had the kitchen and living room upstairs and the bedrooms and workrooms downstairs, which I thought odd. Her lover was an electrician and quietly spoken with a Geordie accent and had eyes more beautiful than the eyes of my enemy.

She didn't make movies back then, but now she does. Back then, I went round to her house often and ate and confessed to various emotions and then we discussed them and she'd pull me apart dipping her chapatti in the curry, or eating her basmati rice with her fingers and telling me that I was unbearably honest. Perceptive. She loved me. She said this with burning eyes. 'I love the way your mind works,' I remember her saying, 'it's strange.'

Her monosyllabic lover nodded, chewing slowly, picking up some raita with her chapatti. My enemy had taught her Geordie lover how to eat like her. When I left I was always aware of sex, even before I'd finished climbing down the bare wooden staircase, the spices still in the air. The complicit smell of cardamom and cumin. It was something to do with the food, the confession. Something to do with me leaving.

Where did I go? I went home and slept. Often I dreamt of my enemy and her lover – the most vivid and frightening dreams of my life. I remember some of those dreams even now – me up on a red roof scrambling. Me in a wedding dress with a thick, swollen tongue unable to speak to my mother. The fascist golfers in their red pullovers climbing up my drainpipe to bang on my bathroom window.

And through every dream, my enemy and her lover making a sudden appearance like Hitchcock in his own movies, as if they were the creators of my dreams. They would be getting on a bus, or rushing out of a shop, or waving from one of those electric caddies at the golf course. The lover with the prematurely grey spiky hair, my enemy with her jet-black hair. Or they would be cleaning my windows.

The two lovers liked to be extremely affectionate to each other in my presence. I don't know why. My enemy would run her hand down her silent lover's back; or she'd rub her thigh and say, 'You rewired this whole house, didn't you, you clever thing?' But when she was touching her, she was looking at me and it was a queer feeling I found in myself. A sort of flipping over inside. Like a fish.

I don't know what made me do it. It is not something I would imagine I would ever do. But then certain types of people cause you to surprise yourself. It is something about them and something about you, the side of you that you were not fully aware of till they revealed it to you. When jealousy is involved, there is no telling the depths, the sinking. No telling, none. I can see that now. It is not regret that has allowed me to see, or even guilt: it is hatred. Cool, hard hatred can afford honesty, generosity. I don't need to misread the truth. I have no passion left for my enemy. She is my enemy; it is simple and it is clear.

Perhaps there is an element of sorrow. I used to love her. I used to love my enemy. Isn't that an awful thought? Doesn't it make you sway and sink, remembering, all those intimacies, compliments, revelations? All that time we shared. All those long, held, meaningful looks. All that laughing. Those tight over-long hugs. I looked right into the depths of her eyes and I thought I loved her. I really did. I thought I could see her soul.

It all started on a wonderful summer's day. A glad-to-be-alive kind of day where the sky had never seemed so generously blue, or the sun so happy. Everything was good. The trees on the streets looked lit up from the inside, holy. I even had clean clothes to match the weather. Cool blue jeans and a white T-shirt. Close-up. I looked at myself in the mirror and wondered if my enemy would fall for me. I put on dark glasses and then I pulled on a cream coloured cap over my dark curls. I put on some lipstick. It was in the days when lipstick was frowned upon by feminists. I wasn't interested in looking beautiful for men. I wanted to look beautiful for my enemy. Of course she wasn't my enemy then, but the present has tainted the past and I can't bring myself to use her name. I can't trust myself. I might hear love in my tone of voice. I might find myself saying her name in the old way. I loved the sound of her name. Foreign and strange on my tongue. I often felt as if I was singing, just saying her name.

So there was the sun, the heat. And there was me stepping down the three steps from my front door and out into the sweltering street. Wide angle. Money in my pocket. Those were the days when no feminist would be seen with a handbag. I admit I found it quite difficult going without a handbag, but liberating too. When you carry a handbag around with you, you might as well carry your own house on your back like a tortoise. A woman's handbag is her house. The keys; the tampons; the lipstick; the fat, spilling purse; the photographs; the pen; the shopping list; the electricity bill in the side-zipped pocket. Loathsome really. I was happy to be stepping down my three steps with a twenty-pound note in the back pocket of my Levi's.

Longshot. I passed the Italian delicatessen on my street – closed with a note on the door saying, 'Gone to Sicily for six weeks,' and I felt pleased Lorenzo was getting his holiday. Last year, money was tight and he'd stayed in London all summer. And I never saw a sadder, longer, Italian face. It seemed his homemade special pastas and breads and pizzas tasted homesick, too, that summer. I passed the vegetable shop where Mrs and Mr Khambatta had just come back from Calcutta. I passed the barber's where several black men were getting their heads shaved for the summer. And all of London looked wonderful to me in all its glory and difference. It made me happy to walk down an ordinary street and see so many vivid, compelling black faces. It made me happy to have my eyes looked into and to look back and to feel part of it all, London, the summer, this day in June.

Cut to me with the flowers. I stopped at the flower shop to buy her flowers. For a moment I briefly worried as to whether her lover might mind. Then I thought I could buy the flowers for both of them, but she would know they were really meant for her. I bought a bunch of pink peonies whose buds were closed tight, closed terribly tight, I imagined, in a kind of sexual spasm. I pictured them bursting open in their house, with the light coming in on the light-wood table and the flowers – stunning – standing at the bottom of the wooden staircase. Like a beautiful still life. She would think of me every time she passed them, how could she not? I breathed in the cool, damp, sweet flower-shop smell as the floral woman wrapped my beautiful bunch of peonies. Her thick arms bare, her face red and vibrantly, viciously healthy.

Everything appeared bigger to me, more important, magnified. I was still slightly hungover from the night before. That might explain, some, not all, of it. The pavement itself sank and came back as I walked upon the hot asphalt. I set off with my peonies and walked as far as the number 73 bus. I loved London buses. I joined the bus at Tottenham High Street outside Tesco. I climbed up the top so that I could see everything. Another longshot. The bus travelled down through Stamford Hill where I saw the Hasidic Jews out in their black hats and ringlets. I felt an odd protectiveness every time I saw a Hasidic Jew, as if the difference was so strong, stronger than my own. More visual, more vivid somehow than my black skin. They looked mysterious to me as if they walked through another time. I could imagine them appearing through mist or fog. I wondered if the clothes, the black hats, the ringlets, the white shirts protected, or not. Through Stamford Hill, down past Stoke Newington's tiny common, round past the fire station and on down

Church Street, past the Abney Park Cemetery, where my enemy and I had had many a walk and talk, where we enjoyed spotting many a man hastily pulling up his fly behind some gravestone, and on down Albion Road on to Newington Green where there was a wonderful Turkish bakery. I stopped there and bought some baklava, some olives, some spinach and feta cheese triangle things, spanakopitas, I think they were called. It's years since I bought them. But I remember everything from this day. Perhaps something in me already knew. Perhaps you anticipate disaster before you are anywhere near it. Surely you must. Why else remember everything in such heartbreaking detail? It can't be the detail of retrospect, of hindsight, can it? Does trauma highlight every moment beforehand with a vivid startling colour, so that you can go back and say 'And then this happened. And then this.' Like a path lit up from behind.

I cut through the back streets of Newington Green into Islington, down Canonbury Park South, Canonbury Place through to Upper Street, right down Islington Park Street, straight across Liverpool Road and into Barnsbury Square where my enemy and her lover sumptuously lived. It was a fifteen-minute walk if I walked at a pace. I did that day. Here's me walking. Cut to my feet, my black boots, walking quickly. As usual, I was anxious to see her. I carried the flowers in the crook of my arm. I felt fairly self-conscious carrying the flowers out in the open streets of London. I thought that they forced people to imagine things about me, to ask questions: Who were the flowers for? What was the occasion?

The flowers were for my enemy who I then adored. The occasion was a party my enemy was throwing for a black American filmmaker from New York. I wasn't a great one for independent arty films but my enemy assured me I was missing out. When she showed clips to me, pointing out the way the film was edited, the techniques, the effect of the music, the atmospheric soundtrack, the choice of lettering for the credits, I loved the whole experience, not because I liked the films (they were often quite dire) but because I was in love with my enemy's voice, and more than that I craved the intimate act of her attention. To sit with her side by side on the sofa whilst she pressed rewind, then still, then play, was something, it really was. To watch her lovely fingers move swiftly and expertly over that remote control. To watch her move the image along, bit by tiny bit. It was so good I was convinced every film she showed me had been made by her.

The film, what was it called, I can't remember, was to have a private screening at the house of my enemy. She had twelve Key People coming she said. They had a small screening room in their basement which the lover had created herself. The screening was to be at seven, but I had said I'd come early to help with the party which was to happen after the screening. So I got there around five o'clock. I was then – I am not now – the sort of person who went early to help, who brought a dish and flowers, who stayed late to clear up. I was creepy; I can admit that now. Very helpful people are creepy, no doubt about it. Why the hell go to someone's house and rub and scrub and make things nice, and sweat and cook and put finishing touches on the table? I suppose I was lonely. It was only my enemy who found me riveting and she had a lover. I flattered myself in thinking that my enemy found her lover dull, and only enjoyed her lover's rather basic touches in bed, but infinitely preferred my consummate intelligence, my sudden leaps of imagination.

So I arrived early, even earlier than they were expecting me. I let myself in with the spare key. I used this key when they were away so I could water their plants and check on their conservatory. I liked sitting in there, when they were travelling, with my feet up and a cup of freshly ground coffee and a newspaper, admiring my enemy's green fingers. I liked looking in their cupboards when they were away. I liked pulling drawers open and looking in. You can tell a lot about people looking in their cupboards. It's like a sneak preview.

As soon as I opened the front door, I heard it. Laughter, if you are not involved yourself, is a terrifying sound. It came from their bedroom. I was going to shout hello, but for some reason I didn't. I just crept in. Their bedroom was second to the right as you came in the front door. The hall was fairly long and narrow, like so many halls in London houses. The door to their bedroom was open. I knew they were expecting me. I mention all this in mitigation. The silent lover was dressed in a sailor suit. Her father had been a sailor-man. There was a photograph of the father from Newcastle on their mantelpiece in the living room, dressed up in all his naval regalia, with badges of honour and such pinned to his breast. There were five-pound notes by the bedside and my enemy was dressed in a red dress, her head back on the bed, laughing. Her dress was pulled up and the sailor's trousers were pulled down. Something was sticking out of them. That was all I saw. In a split second perhaps. There was a lot of quite aggressive movement from the taciturn lover, and a lot of silly laughter coming from my enemy who was perhaps having trouble taking the whole thing seriously. Her lover was having no such trouble; I caught the side of her face: it was dark and serious.

I don't remember the next bit properly. I know I went to the kitchen, climbing softly up the stairs. I know I started cooking, chopping like I'd been taught to chop when I worked in a restaurant; fast, keeping the sharpest of knives close to the wood board and moving along from the front to the back, viciously, expertly quickly. Greek parsley shattered into tiny pieces. Quite a deep, almost a jade, green. I tried not to listen. I put the radio on low, Radio 3. Their radio was permanently tuned to Radio 3. Someone was singing some sad opera song. The voice took me away from their noise for a few moments.

They came into the kitchen with completely different expressions on their faces at five-thirty. My enemy looked ashamed and soft as if she knew she had hurt me. She ruffled her hand through my hair and said, 'Oh thanks, Beverley, for getting started.' I loved it when she said my name. Although she had lived in England for most of her life, her accent had something extra, her stresses and intonations were slightly different. She stressed the last bit of my name. Her lover picked up one of my spinach and cheese triangles and ate it in one bite.

'Nice. Did you bring these?' she said. Then she stuck her middle finger in the bowl of hummus, that I'd sprinkled with paprika, and licked her finger. The gesture was really saying, *Fuck you.* She stared right at me as she did it and then she said, 'All right?'

'You're cutting it a bit fine if people are arriving at six-thirty,' I said.

'No sweat. Everything's under control,' the lover said looking over at my enemy with the sailor's stare on her face. 'Isn't it, sweetheart?'

I think that was it. That was the final blow. I exploded. 'What do you two think you are playing at! Do you think I'm your skivvy, come to get your party food ready whilst you two play at sailors? Don't look shocked. You meant me to see.' I was shaking with anger. My enemy put her arm round me and said, 'Come here.' And I went. I followed her through to their living room where Nina Simone was singing, *Oh Baltimore Ain't it hard just to live.* I sat down next to her on the sofa and I laid my head on her breast. 'When is Beverley going to get a lover?' she said.

I got up, calmed for a moment by that superior closeness, by feeling her breath on my neck, her hands on my shoulder. I didn't really want more than that. That was enough. But it was clearly too much for the lover. She looked as if she would like to get me on my own in one of those narrow Islington mews one night.

As I left the room, I saw the pair of them exchange a look. I remember it because it puzzled me. What were they saying to each other? She's tougher than we think? She's crazy? We've gone too far? Let's play some more? Whatever it was, they were in complete agreement. I went back into the kitchen and continued making tabbouleh the way a Lebanese friend had taught me. I chopped the parsley and the mint. I soaked the bulgar wheat. But I couldn't get the image out of my head. The lover in the sailor's suit. It all seemed obscene to me. It seemed disrespectful to her father. My enemy was too innocent for all of that. She needed a nice girl like me.

At the party that night, the Key People appeared to me like an odd cast of characters full of poise and presence and posture, talking a language I didn't understand. I fought with myself not to feel stupid, but I stayed in the corner and said very little to anybody. I sipped at a glass of wine and tried to look interesting, but nobody was drawn to me. I didn't even eat any of the food I had prepared, though I noticed it was going down well. I overheard my enemy say to one of them, 'Don't mind Beverley, she's always like that. A bit shy.' And I fumed. They were mentioning names of people and films I had never heard of. I liked thrillers, film noirs, spaghetti westerns. I liked Bette Davis, the Godfather movies and *Calamity Jane*. I loved Julie Andrews. I loved the scene in *The Sound of Music* where Captain von Trapp tells Maria she can stay and Maria claps her hands to herself three times on the stairs. I didn't imagine anybody would want to talk about any of these people to me. I did try. I said to a woman with very dark dyed-black hair, 'Do you like *Calamity Jane* at all?' and she sort of stared at me and said. 'She's fun. Look I have to get a refill,' and never came back. All this was out of my depth. I couldn't wait for them to go and for me to have my enemy to myself. I noticed Lover Girl was getting drunker and drunker and her Geordie accent thicker and thicker till she sounded like someone out of *When the Boat Comes In.* I could hear it like a soundtrack inside my own head. Finally they all left, in twos or threes. Nobody else offered to help clear up. The very idea! The lover was stoatin' about the place, unsteady on her pins. I watched her clumsy movements in slow motion. Then she passed out on the sofa. That left me and my enemy, washing plates, glasses, putting drinks away. I was standing at the sink washing the dishes when she put her arms around me from behind me and turned me round. She pulled my hair towards her and kissed me, passionately.

It was like the kiss in *Double Indemnity*, when they first fall for each other. It was risky. Dangerous. Then she took my hand and led me downstairs to their bed. I did not initiate anything. I swear on my mother's life I didn't. The film she made was a lie. I didn't even have a part to play when I look back on it. She wrote the script and she directed. I think it was her idea of fun.

We went to bed and she took off all my clothes. Pulled my jeans down, took off my pants, my bra, till I was completely naked lying next to her fully clothed. I went to say something and she put her finger to my lip and said 'Ssssssh. Don't talk, my darling, don't spoil it.' Then she took off her red dress, slowly. Oh God, very slowly. She bent down and put her fingers in my mouth and moved them out and in, so so slowly. I didn't speak. I collapsed into her, I pulled her towards me. I couldn't stop myself. I had been waiting too long.

It was only when we had finished that I noticed her lover standing by the door, watching. I broke out into a cold sweat. I pulled the white sheet around my naked body. I felt so revealed. Captured in the one shot. The expression on her lover's face was not what I would have expected. She looked excited, not angry. Aroused, not agitated. It came to me in a flash that they had planned this whole thing. That the lover had pretended to fall asleep. That she'd wanted to watch. That my enemy had made a total fool out of me. She didn't love me. She didn't care about me at all. She just wanted to humiliate me.

I saw myself get up, pull on my jeans, pull on my T-shirt. I saw myself walk up the bare wooden staircase in my bare feet. I saw a close-up of my own feet on the top stair. As I turned the corner towards the kitchen, I swung around and saw the two of them standing at the bottom of the stairs. The lover had my enemy pushed up against the wall and was kissing her violently. The kitchen door opened and I walked through it. The mugs were swinging from the rail. The pans and pots were shaking from their silver hooks. The terracotta tile floor was too damn red.

I picked up the small sharp vegetable knife. I saw my hand do it. It is true. My own hand. It looked to me as if for a moment there was nothing on the Formica except my hand and that knife. I remember all of this too vividly. I remember the strangeness of carrying out actions without any feelings. I remember how heavy my feet felt as I walked slowly down the stairs. One step at a time. Absurdly, I noticed the sheen on the pine staircase.

Strange how big moments are always very fast and very slow simultaneously. Looking back at them, you can see yourself doing every single thing as if in slow motion, yet in reality, in the heart of the terrible moment, everything happens too swiftly, so fast as to be out of control. I have never worked that out.

I must have rushed at her with the knife. I could not stick a knife in her back; my upbringing wouldn't allow that, too cowardly and underhand. I grabbed the lover and swung her round. 'Take this!' I said and stabbed the knife straight into her side. Then the moment rewound itself, a screaming whirr backwards and I saw myself stabbing her in her side. She grunted and moved her hand to the wounded place and then fell on to the floor. She lay on their Turkish carpet with the blood seeping out of her. It worked beautifully, it hurt her, but it was not lethal. All flesh, no organs. I got a suspended sentence for mitigating circumstances; being previously so clean, so law-abiding helped, I think. It was quite a cause célèbre our little trial. It attracted headlines that made it very difficult for me to bring my pint of milk in or to go to my corner shop. *Lesbian Love Triangle* and other such awful headlines. Do people really *think* like that or is it just the tabloids?

I let the knife fall out of my hand and on to the floor. I felt like collapsing myself from the effort of it all, from all that love and emotion. I couldn't credit myself. I was the last person in the world to pull such a stunt.

The lover had a minor stab wound and recovered quickly. A few years later when their movie came out, *All About Beatrice*, I went along and was horrified at how they portrayed the character that was clearly myself. They had got me all wrong. They really were stupid. It infuriated me that they were still playing around with me in this way, that they underestimated my intelligence. They had me down as some geek, some weirdo, some lonely lesbian that had tried to come between them. In their movie, the character that is so obviously and revoltingly me, tries to contrive a whole relationship out of one drunken kiss. She reads too much into things. She is pathetic, clumsy, dyslexic, lonely. The other two feel sorry for her and she takes advantage. She starts to creep in and tries to take over their lives. They kick her out after the kiss.

They would never have dreamt that I would get my revenge. It is private, my revenge. I would never show it to the public. But it is sweet. I know they have seen me once or twice hanging outside their house with my camcorder, filming them going in, filming them closing the curtains of 10 Barnsbury Square. I know they suspect it is me who rings, then hangs up. Once I heard my enemy say, 'Beverley?

Bev, is that you?' She sounded really quite unnerved. I have sometimes called in the middle of the night because I remembered my enemy was an insomniac.

Once or twice, I've actually been right to the front door when I was positive they were out. I've checked by the old cracked flower pot for the spare keys only to find them missing. A pity, because I would have taken pleasure in going into their bedroom and changing their sheets, folding the white sheet expertly under the mattress like I'd been taught at Homerton Hospital. I'd have liked the idea of them returning to a clean bed. They would have got my message. The small window at the front was closed. Of course one day it might be left open and I would have no trouble explaining to the neighbours why I was climbing in. The neighbours know me.

If I was ever to make a movie, I would call it that, 10 Barnsbury Square. It would be about three women. It would attract controversy. It would not be your wishy-washy arty lesbian movie. It would be a huge and unexpected hit. I quite fancy trying my hand at it. But I've heard you need contacts for such things, to get started. You need Key People.

Strange though, how that sentence of hers still rings. *When is Beverley going to find a lover?* Before that night, I had never had sex with anyone. I was always waiting for the right moment. Since that night, the right moment has never come again. Her lips were so very soft, so surprising.

Married women

Isabel has left her husband for me. The others never managed to get out. The house, the garden, the kids, the meals, the plates and bowls, the money, the joint accounts, the car, the spare room, the piano, the paintings, the books, the dog, the goldfish were all more than I had to offer. I left them to it in the end, Harriet, Jessica, Lana. Oh, they wanted me to keep meeting them when the husbands were away, to keep up the furtive, dangerous sex. But I began to feel like a plaything and my life didn't feel real. That's absurd, I know, for a life not to feel real, but that's how I felt. Going home to my room in the shared flat; having hardly any money, knowing that the mistress of the moment was tucking into a lovely posh dinner with side dishes and good wine while I was chomping a curry or a Chinese or a chip buttie. I never cooked but I could microwave. I was an expert at piercing through the film of ready-made meals. Relationships had degenerated to the extent that my selfish slobbish flatmates cooked for themselves. There was the indignity of having to suffer little labels in the fridge with people's names stuck to a carton of hummus or a large tub of live yoghurt. Talk about style! I rose above the whole squalid business and never bought anything much except tea and coffee. I drank both black to avoid autographing a pint of milk.

I finished with Harriet when she wouldn't even go for a drink with me because it was too much of a risk and she feared husband Martin was suspicious. With Jessica, when . . . well, I never really did find out why it finished with Jessica. With Lana. Oh Lana, that was the worst experience of the lot. She actually wanted to involve her husband. She wanted me to go to bed with the pair of them in the end. And he, the sick fuck, was up for it. Lana was a beautiful black woman married to an ugly podgy white man. But he was Sensitive and Gentle and Adoring, supporting Lana through every adventure, including me. Lana was the only one to confess to her husband, to Tell All. I didn't know it at the time but apparently Lana told husband Iain right after our first night and then hid from me the fact that he knew. How weird is that? When I found out that he had known all along, I was furious. It meant that Lana's secret was with Iain and not with me. In a peculiar way, *they* were the pair having the affair. They used me to give their bloody union a jump-start. A kick up the married arse. That killed it for me. I didn't want Iain in on the know. I could imagine him imagining us. It gave me the creeps. What is it with men and lesbians? Why do they like the idea so much?

Secrecy. I loved the danger, the rushed whispered phone calls, meeting incognito, the fear of somebody one of us knew turning up in an unexpected place. The fear of the husband coming home earlier than anticipated. The fear of an alibi exploding. The fear of me leaving my watch behind, or my ring. The fear of a letter being discovered. (To my horror, Harriet burnt my letters as soon as she received them. 'I can't have any proof,' she said.)

You have to be clever to have a successful secret affair; you have to be ahead of the game, to plan and anticipate every little thing. Deceit uses up a lot of your energy. Lying makes you slim. I lost the equivalent of two bags of sugar with each of my married women (or eight packs of butter depending on the way you weigh things up.) The more I lied, the thinner and more ambitious looking I became. I was a fucking expert; I'd tell my married women what to do. The whole secrecy thing thrilled me. People might say that there was something wrong with me always snatching somebody's spouse. Well of course there was! But life was delicious. Once Jessica came to meet me in disguise. Oh, it was so exciting. Her hair was up and under a hat I had never seen. Her lipstick was very red. She was wearing a new long raincoat and it was turned up at the collar. She had dark glasses on although it wasn't even the summer. We sat in a dark corner at the back of a pub and drank Bloody Marys.

Of course Lana was genuine, lovely and wanted everybody to share and appreciate each other. The poor thing didn't understand that that wasn't possible. Lana might love him, but I didn't. Something about the way he talked grated, the way he hesitated and said a very long 'Yeeeesss'. The creamy, unctuous way he had of trying to please. The idea of being in bed with Iain and Lana together turned me off Lana. The whole reason she chose to tell me that Iain knew was at Iain's instigation! To lure me into a threesome. It was outrageous. I was hurt. Things hadn't been happening the way I'd thought they'd been happening at all. No more married women I promised myself. They are just too selfish. Lana was going to be my last.

I threw myself into my work, the pathology and histopathology of a systemic granuloma in *Sparus aurata*. The poor fish had a sort of chronic, inflammatory disease of the internal organs. I found urinary stones in the fishes' kidneys and bladder. Oh yes, fish do have bladders. I was fascinated to be discovering tyrosine urolites which were quite unique. They had been found in caught-wild fry in the Bardawil lagoon.

My work had bored all of my married women except Harriet who could listen for ages to in-depth descriptions of fish diseases. I was still a student, a superior super-student, going for my Ph.D at the Institute of Aquaculture, University of Stirling. I had been studying for seven years to get this elusive Ph.D when it should have really taken me three. If I'd kept my head down and not let one married woman after another come along and distract me from my studies, I would have been Doctor Winters.

The married women around the Stirling area of Bridge of Allan, Dollar, Callendar, were quite open. Much more so than women in big cities like London or Glasgow. I'd lived in both and hadn't had nearly such a good time. Perhaps it was being in a smaller place and close to a university that did it: the university life seeped out of the campus and into the town, allowed grown adults to embrace changes into their lives in the way that students do. Cataclysmic, dynamic, revolutionary.

I shared a flat with two much younger students, two fervent undergraduates, Phillip and Madhu. Both were members of the Anti-Nazi League and the men's consciousness-raising group. Phil was sociology; Madhu was English. Both were sweet but irritating because they believed they were the first people on the planet to believe in anything: world peace, an end to racism, equality for women in the workplace, an end to dialectical materialism. All I believed in was the joys and the pleasures of married women. At that time not a day went past without me blessing the state of marriage for all it had given me.

How it went with Harriet.

Harriet and I both attended a meeting and our eyes met across the crowded room. When the eyes click in that wonderful, knowing way there is no cliché. Harriet had a thick head of healthy, auburn hair. Her eyes were gleaming, shining with a kind of new excitement. It is true that women find each other more exciting than men find each other, that they go about the place charged and thrilled in each other's presence. It is no different either when you look at girls and boys playing. Girls have so much fun together. It's a sobering thought, but even being in bed with one of the finest of my married women was nothing to that feverish, heady excitement I felt when I was a girl with my best friend, running down a hill, screaming.

I went back with Harriet to her house and she poured me a gin and tonic, laughed and said, 'I can hardly believe this is happening. You seem so familiar and I don't even know you.' A gift of a line, a freebie. The rest was not difficult. Harriet's husband was actually up the stairs that first night, in bed with a terrible flu, feeling what Harriet called 'a ghastly, unattractive self-pity'. So perhaps if it hadn't been for husband Martin having the flu, the whole affair with Harriet wouldn't have started. There is something so unsexy about illness; I sympathized with Harriet when she said, 'Men make such a fuss. You'd think they were dying.' I'm never ill. We could hear him coughing upstairs as we kissed. A cough that was so rough it sounded as if he was trying to throw up his voice box. 'Should we be doing this?' I said for form's sake. 'I don't think so,' Harriet laughed, 'still it is only the once.'

'Only the once,' I said, hurt because Harriet was hugely attractive, warm, round with an easy flirtatious laugh. I wanted to bury myself in her, to lay my head on her breasts and sleep, just sleep. 'Well, we'll see,' she said with the terrible confidence of the married middle-class woman.

It wasn't just that once with Harriet. I wish now it had been. I wish I hadn't been so stupid as to keep going back for more. One day, I went round with a bunch of flowers and she said, 'Oh I can't accept these. Martin will want to know who they are from.'

'Well, tell him you bought them for yourself,' I said, impatiently.

'Oh, I can't lie like that,' she said. I snorted.

'You can't lie? You're telling a lie the whole time!'

'Not that kind of lie,' Harriet said. 'I'm quite careful about what's believable and what's not. I daren't risk anything else. I think Martin would be quite violent if he found out about us.'

'So I can't even buy you a present?'

'I'm afraid not. That's the deal.' Harriet said, smiling and ruffling my hair. 'Anyway,' she said, 'I don't need presents, I've got you.' For some reason the whole petty episode made me feel sour and sulky. It made me feel trapped. Other people could do these things without thinking, buy flowers, write a letter, stay the night. What upset me most was that Harriet really wasn't bothered. She couldn't care less whether I bought her flowers or not. I don't think she needed to be liked. I worked out that although she was drawn to me and loved our sexual life, she wasn't really interested in much else about me except for what I was doing with my fish. This made our post-sex conversation a bit limited. 'Tell me about your fish,' she would say, lying back as I babbled on about lesions and losses that have occurred sporadically amongst older fish, about tests made to isolate a primary viral, bacterial or fungal agent that had yielded negative results. Harriet never looked at me with more love or admiration than when I was talking about my fish.

Then one day I was at home in my digs that I stayed in for an eternity, the upstairs flat of 24

Abercromby Place, Stirling, when the bell rang and Harriet came thundering up the stairs. We always left the front door unlocked. Nothing of value to nick. 'I'm really sorry, Kim, but I can't see you anymore. Martin has become really suspicious and is making my life hell.'

'Leave him then,' I said, 'Come away with me,'

'What here?' she waved her arms around the tatty kitchen, at the ripped lino, the ancient tobacco-stained wallpaper, the old fierce gas cooker, the kitchen cupboards, there since the sixties, hanging off their hinges. 'It doesn't need to be here,' I said. 'We could get our own place.' She smiled at me as if she was not sure whether or not I was serious. 'Oh come on. We just wanted to have some fun, and now it's not fun, so it has to stop. Don't call me anymore.' And she left, down the stairs, quick, quick in her haughty high heels. I watched her from the window getting into her silver BMW and drive off. 'Are you OK?' Phillip said to me that evening. He must have taken pity on me because he invited me to share his sad stir-fried supper. I'd gone to the off licence round the corner and bought us a bottle of Chianti. It was the only thing that made the food bearable. I'd take a nibble of noodle, then a swig of wine. 'Fine,' I said, slurping my wine at a much quicker rate than Phillip. 'Fine. You know life. It can be a bit of a downer.'

But a week later we were back to whispers on the phone, to Harriet saying she was sorry and she missed me, to wild grateful sex up against the wall in a Ladies toilet. Harriet was older than I was. Forty-nine. All of my mistresses were older than I was. I didn't fancy younger women at all. People say that women come into themselves around this age and it is true. Harriet was blooming. Her looks were still there; they hadn't yet collapsed. She hadn't got jowls or thick hips. No, she was shapely and beautiful and every time I looked at her I couldn't believe my luck. But when the whole ridiculous business started up again – Martin's terrible paranoia, Harriet's guilt – I had to get out to save my sanity. It was starting to eat away at me. Harriet made it plain that Martin and she still had an active sex life. I didn't like thinking about it. It was too much in my face. I was starting to have problems sleeping at night. I'd wish that I could spend one whole night with Harriet. Just one whole night. That time, the last time, I said to her, 'It's over,' and meant it. Finito.

I bumped into Harriet once, coming out of the Central library and it was still there, the desire thudded right through my body till I hurt. The rain was lashing down. Harriet, Harriet, Harriet. Why did I put myself through it? I liked the way my married mistresses dressed. I liked the way they smelled. I liked their wedded bosoms. I liked their soft cared-for skin. Their clean hair. I liked the ring on their finger and their nice nails. They did things that dykes didn't: they put powderpuffs under their breasts, or they wore camisoles, or fancy knickers, flimsy bras. They wore lipstick and perfume and foundation cream. Perhaps I just hadn't met the right lesbians, but the ones I knew then were rough and ready and predictable. Oh yes – same kind of short haircut, same trousers and jackets with pockets, same loose baggy T-shirts, or big checked shirts, same,

same, same. They had a look about them that was so easy to identify if you were in the know. I didn't like that. I couldn't help myself. I didn't fancy dykes. There wasn't enough tension in it for me. I liked the agonizing struggle of not knowing – yes, no, yes, no, yes, yes please. Harriet and I gave each other a look that said we used to love each other once, we don't now, do we; do we? And moved on. I noticed the rain was running down her face. She went into the library with books under her arms and I was left walking down the wet steps into Dumbarton Road. I crossed over, walking slowing in the rain up Glebe Avenue towards home. I wanted her to follow me. If she had followed me, I might have swept her up again in my arms and kissed her, softly, slowly. Not to be.

Then there was Lana.

I don't want to think about Lana. I can't think about Lana. Don't let me go there. No, no, no, no, no.

The drama with Jessica.

Jessica had been married eight years and had never, in her words, 'so much as looked at somebody'. She and husband Alastair were compatible, companionable, enjoyed each other's company, one could read a book and the other a newspaper in perfect harmonious silence. So Jessica was luminous with guilt but easily the most passionate of my wives. I found her self-recriminations dull and wouldn't indulge them. But the guilt plus the fear of discovery made for an absolute whirlwind of an affair. We should have known it would end up how it did.

Alastair was the local minister and Jessica lived

with him in the manse. It was up at the manse that we first met. I was there for a cup of tea and a discussion about a charity I was involved in at the time. Jessica poured me the tea and then sat down to talk to me and became all tongue-tied and awkward. After that, I contrived one reason after another to get back to the manse. The next visit confirmed my suspicions. Jessica blushed when she saw me and again there were strange charged pauses in our conversation. You could call them spiritual pauses. Holy moments.

It is a strange way to go on. I felt so attracted to her I was frightened in her presence. I found myself swallowing hard. My hands were hot. I felt uncomfortable and alarmed. But I enjoyed it, the fear, and those odd silences where it seemed as if Jessica and I both hung from a beam in the manse, swinging. It was lovely that nerve-wracking courting with Jessica. We drew it out for six weeks before anything happened. Then one day, it did.

We were alone in the manse and Jessica leaned towards me when she poured my tea. I took a sip, then put my cup and saucer down on the low table. I turned towards her and she was waiting in that way that people wait for their lives to come along without them doing very much except leaning slightly forward. Her eyes searched my face. I could tell she had never ever done this before. We kissed, tentatively at first, then more passionately. And there was no going back.

Of all places to have sex with a married woman, the manse was my favourite. It was a beautiful house, had a lovely conservatory and the walls throbbed with religion. It was so wrong to do it there it was right. Jessica would say, 'Not here,' and then she would collapse into me as if she couldn't walk. She told me she had never had sex like it. She was unprepared. She had no idea. She finally understood what all the fuss was about. She was overwhelmed. I was the only one who could make her cry, who could make her lose herself and call out into the deep darkness. Each time she looked as if she was being born again, her face so new and fresh and astonished.

Jessica had short dark brown hair and was as tall as me. We looked good together. She said to me once, while we looked at ourselves in the mirror. 'Isn't it funny how I suit you better than I suit Alastair?' Then she kissed me and I saw her look at our reflection to try and see what our snog looked like.

Jessica's guilt grew and grew until she told me we couldn't meet at the manse anymore. This made things difficult for us, but not impossible. A friend of mine gave me a set of spare keys to her place. She lived on her own and was hardly ever there. My place was out of the question: too messy, two undergraduates sleeping half the day away. We couldn't afford for anyone to see us. One day I went to meet Jessica at my friend's ground floor flat as planned but she didn't show up. I was worried something had happened to her, but we had a rule I must not now ring the manse. I must always wait for her calls. The next day, I went back to our place, well it felt like our place when we were there, at our usual time, in the hope that Jessica would be there. I did this for three more days. Finally, when I could stand it no longer, I phoned the manse hoping I would get Jessica. But the husband answered, so I hung up. I tried again the following day. That time Jessica answered but as soon as I spoke, she said, 'I can't talk to you,' and hung up. In a fit of fury, I walked round to the manse when I knew her husband would be out at his Tuesday night meeting. Jessica opened the door an inch. 'I'm sorry, Kim. There's no easy way of doing this. Don't come back.' She closed the door in my face. I rang the bell. Again and again. 'You're disturbing the children,' she shouted through the letterbox. 'Go away!' She seemed frightened.

'What's happened?' I said. 'Can you just talk to me for ten minutes!'

'No, now go!' she shouted. I could hear she was crying. 'Just leave me!' I walked away, walking backwards, still looking at the house in case she changed her mind and opened the door. She didn't. The manse door stayed shut. I ran the rest of the way home. I don't know how long I cried for, long enough for my features to distort and my voice to sound hoarse. Why hadn't Jessica at least written me a note? How could she say all those things to me and do this?

During my days with Jessica, I would get the bus out to the university. Ours was a winter affair; I'd often see the Wallace monument loom like a ghost through the mist, the moody Ochils in the distance. I'd get off the bus and walk up the steep hill. Then I'd go to the Pathfoot building and continue my research. I'd type up my results of gross pathology. White deposits evident in the anterior chamber. Skin lesions on the tail. The kidney bulges into the abdomen and nodular lesions are present in the spleen and liver. I'd type away quite fast. This kind of work was easy for me, but it didn't engage me. My mind wandered off the studies of the liver, heart, gut, the mesenteries and muscles and on to Jessica. I thought I could have been happy with Jessica. I'd see her beautiful face swim in front of my fish. So I made myself a promise. Never, ever again. In no time, I decided, I would finish writing up my pathology and histopathology and complete my dissertation. I could then move on. Go and live in a city. Somewhere.

I know I wasn't even looking for anything when I met Isabel. I was keeping my head down and walking quickly along the corridors of the university when I literally bumped into her.

Isabel was in the English department. At the moment I met her she was the head. The head rotated, she told me. I liked the idea of a head rotating. I pictured it, going round and round and round on a revolving plate like something from a bloodier age. I had gone along to one of her lectures in the Logie theatre the previous semester. Occasionally, I liked to do this, attend odd lectures of different disciplines, partly because I liked the strangeness of it, sitting in a room with students I didn't know and partly because I liked to increase my knowledge of things. Isabel's lecture was on D. H. Lawrence. She was very entertaining. I told her all this in the corridor and she asked me what I was doing now. The fish pathology seemed to intrigue and relieve her. She didn't want me to be another English student. She told me I must come round sometime, and meet her husband. He liked fishing in his spare time. I nodded and I knew.

It was important to me to avoid getting to know Isabel's husband. If I knew too much about the life; the dinners, the wines, the interests, the meaningful records, the favourite restaurant, pub, the Sunday walk, the TV programmes they enjoyed, the movie they had just seen, the holiday they were planning, the plants they had just planted, the photograph they'd just had framed, I found it profoundly off-putting, sickening. Marriage. What a dull stupid business it all is: choosing tiles and carpet colours and curtains and wallpaper. I swore I would never find any of that kind of thing interesting. I thought it was all beneath me. The very idea of going to the theatre or the movies or on holiday or into town or out to the country always or mostly always with the spouse appalled me. The notion that every night you might want to get into the same bed and sleep with the same person! Marriage and its secrets and its hypocrisy and its failure, its failure to stay fresh, to keep the passion burning, to keep the heart beating, the shyness, the surprise. Marriage was one big con for people not brave enough to love at the deep end, or the hot end, or the sharp end. You started off two people and ended up as one. You fetched up wearing each other's expressions. You finished up the same, sharing the same glasses to watch a foreign film. Save me! I used to clown to my friends, save me from the cul-de-sac marriage is. Don't let me go there.

One day Isabel and I were in bed and she told me my eyes were dark and that I wasn't getting enough sleep. 'You should drink less and smoke less,' she said. 'I worry about you.' I was shocked. 'You don't get to bed early enough,' she said. I tried to work out what was unusual about Isabel saying this. Then it came to me: not one of my married women had ever really cared about me. Not one of them had ever asked me how I was, or what I had been doing. My life bored them; it was of no interest or consequence. I kissed Isabel and drew her towards me. 'I don't want to go,' Isabel said. 'I hate leaving you and going back to him. I can't stand the sight of him now. It's not his fault but all of his little habits are getting on my nerves. Even the way he eats! Especially the way he eats. I'm starting to resent him and he knows something is wrong. He's even asked me what's wrong. I haven't had the guts to tell him the truth.' I stroked her hair. I didn't want her to go either. 'What a farce marriage is!' I said. Isabel ignored me. 'I'd like to look after you,' she said suddenly. 'You need looking after. I could be your wife. Wouldn't you like a wife, wouldn't you like me to be your wife?' I thought she was joking at first till I looked at her face. It was quite still and serious. Her eyes held mine for the longest time. I felt myself melt, I let myself go. It was the most shocking moment of my entire life. I knew right there and then that I wanted Isabel to be my wife. To have and to hold. 'Don't play with me,' I said, pulling myself back from the dream. 'I'm not.' Isabel said. 'I'll leave him. I want to be with you. I love you.' She stroked the tears away from my cheeks. 'You're crying,' she said. Then she started to cry herself.

And now here we are, Isabel and I, we've just agreed on the colour of the kitchen tiles. We both like white plates. We've chosen a sunshine yellow for the walls; next weekend we're going to paint it together which should be fun. After that we're going to tackle the bedroom. We both fancy something quite sexy, maybe a light violet on the walls. It is surprising and exciting to discover that we have similar taste. We love shopping for our home. Every single new thing we buy is bought with love, the kind of love I would have never imagined you could feel for things, for objects. Buying new sheets for our bed, or a picture for our hall, or a lamp for our living room, or just a simple cushion fills me with an intense happiness, the like of which I have never ever known. We haven't got the money yet for doing up the bathroom, but you have to take things one step at a time when you're married. You can't just rush things and expect your house to be perfect overnight. I've heard other married people say as much. We're talking about getting a cat from a rescue home. Isabel likes cats; so do I. We're not dog people. We don't go out all that much in the evenings. I love it when Isabel cooks for me and we have a good bottle of wine; later, we might read and listen to Elgar or Bach or Shostakovich if we want something strenuous and exciting. Sometimes if we are both tired, we watch *Prime Suspect*. We both love *Prime*.

We don't live in Stirling anymore. Isabel's husband was vicious over the break up and at one point pushed her down the stairs. He still rings in the middle of the night, drunk and ranting until one of us hangs up. It has done the poor man's head in. His wife leaving him for another woman. Isabel said it has made him shrink. Shame.

I couldn't think of being unfaithful now that I am with Isabel. I don't so much as look at anybody. She wouldn't either, I don't think. I am so much happier. We practise our vows together. We say them to each other in the dark at night. In sickness and in health. Kiss. For richer or poorer. Kiss. Better or worse. Kiss. I want to do it properly. I want a minister to join us together. I want my friends to come and my family. I know my parents could be persuaded eventually. Isabel says, 'I'm yours, Kim. We don't really need an official ceremony.' But I disagree. Now that I'm with Isabel, I think that ceremonies are important. Extremely important. I want the bit of paper, too. The minute the law changes, I will be down there, at the church or the registry office saying *I do* and looking straight into my Isabel's beautiful eyes.

Physics and Chemistry

Before Physics and Chemistry's life altered completely and forever one morning in June, Chemistry added a couple of drops of vinegar to the small pan, then slid Physics's egg in, slowly. Poaching was a talent. Physics hadn't bothered trying to poach an egg for about ten years. Even on school mornings Physics and Chemistry made sure they had a good breakfast. These days the division of domestic tasks in the house was quite simple: Chemistry poached eggs, roasted chicken, made the salad dressing, sent the cards, dusted, chose the new curtains, or the shade of emulsion; Physics made the bed, put the bin out, changed the light bulbs, serviced the car, wrapped the presents, did the ironing, wired the plugs. Chemistry washed, Physics dried. Neither believed in dishwashers – though, at home, in private, they marvelled at those in their staff room who claimed the dishwasher had saved their marriage.

Physics and Chemistry smiled small scientific smiles in the staff room when the subject of marriage came up. One of the more insensitive teachers, Mrs

Fife (home economics, big apron) once famously said to Chemistry:

'You are not the kind of spinster I feel embarrassed talking about marriage to. I mean, I would have thought you could have easily got married, if you'd wanted to.'

In the staff room that day, quite some time ago now, there was a gigantic embarrassed silence. It seeped round the staff room making everybody blush. The odd thing was that everyone, the history teacher, the English teacher, the maths teacher, the PE teacher, felt a peculiar mixture of glee and shame, just like they might have for a member of their own family, for Mrs Fife's faux pas. She herself was blissfully unaware. Almost charmingly so.

'Oh dear, have I put my foot in it?' she finally said when the big wallop of silence was too much even for her not to notice. It was down to Chemistry to summon all of her generosity and say, 'I think I prefer the term single woman, it sounds more modern.' Physics fumed by the kettle, stirring her coffee.

When Mrs Fife made her gaffes, when pupils referred to Physics and Chemistry as *the Science Spinsters,* Physics always, always pretended not to hear. Physics was tall with long bones in her face, a long nose, large hands, and thick short hair, greying now. She had more hair than she would wish around her top lip. Recently, she noticed, it was even more of a presence than ever, perhaps it was her age. Still, there was nothing she could do about it; she was not going to subject herself to electrolysis, she'd heard that was painful and Physics hated pain. A coward, pain-wise, Chemistry said so. Physics had never been in hospital or had anything much wrong with her, but the slightest ache would have her moaning for days. Physics overheard one pupil say to another, 'Look at that moustache. She looks like a man.' And again she had stared straight ahead. Every day, in her own silent way, Physics kept something to herself.

At home in their Wimpey house, in Gleneagles Gardens, off the main Kirkintilloch Road, not too far from Bishopbriggs High School, where they both taught, Physics pulled the strings to shut the curtains, and put her slippers on. Physics and Chemistry had identical moccasin slippers, which they replaced every Christmas. At home, slippers on, fire lit – a fake gas fire that attempted to look like a real one, but never really fooled anybody – the *Scotsman* in hand, Physics felt herself physically relaxing. Most of the long school day, she stayed unlit and dangerous as one of Chemistry's experiments, the potential to blow up, to turn suddenly pink, to sparkle and spit, never far from her surface. At home, Physics would tell Chemistry some of the things she had pretended not to hear that day and Chemistry would tell Physics things back; sympathy and hilarity bubbled between them; and Chemistry's eyes lit up like a blue flame.

Some nights they sat at dinner – Physics in her chair by the kitchen door and Chemistry in the one opposite, and the weight of all the things they'd listened to in silence moved around them like molecules. The dinner in the middle of the table, the organic vegetables cooked in lemon grass and coconut oil, sat between them, a bright, colourful wok of strange ingredients as far as Physics was concerned. If Physics had her way, she would have a roast lamb, two veg and mashed potatoes and a nice wee jug of gravy. She ate all these unfamiliar, oddly upsetting, foods out of love. Her very palette had transformed since Chemistry's culinary habits had turned foreign a few years back. Chemistry always wanted to do things differently. Physics had to be forced to change. In the kitchen, the flushed pleasure on Chemistry's cheeks, the brightness of her voice and eyes, when she held out a spoon and said try this and pronounced some strange words like *gadoh gadoh* or *sayur lemak* or *sambal tauco*, made Physics want to drop to her knees with love and disappointment.

Physics was not an enthusiastic woman herself, but she admired the quality in others, marvelled at the way Chemistry could stretch her arms out and shout *Yippee*, or do a little skip or clap her hands loudly together and shriek *Yes!* when Evonne Goolagong won Wimbledon. Physics's mother had never smiled much; she thought that people who grinned widely were ignorant or idiotic; Physics's father had wanted a boy. She had never been hugged in her life until she met Chemistry. Even now she was uncomfortable if Chemistry touched her anywhere but in bed.

They sat at dinner, Chemistry boldly eating her Malaysian food with clever chopsticks; Physics clinging to a fork. A bottle of chilled Alsace in a bucket on the table. This wine bucket was another Christmas present from Chemistry to Physics, so that they could have, at home, a semblance of a restaurant. Why go out? Why ever go out? Most nights, Chemistry cooked. At weekends, they had special meals with wine. Physics always opened and poured the wine. During the week, they had quick meals with water or a cup of tea. After dinner, they did their marking. After marking, they'd watch the news. After the news, they might watch one of their favourite programmes, *Frost* or *Morse*, *The Street* or *Panorama*. Usually Chemistry would fall asleep on the chair and Physics would smoke a cigarette outside the back door. Chemistry was an ex-smoker, the worst kind. Physics usually waited till Chemistry nodded off, sneaked out of the back door and smoked one or two Benson and Hedges. She enjoyed figuring out the constellations on such smoking nights on her own back door-step, puffing upwards towards the brilliant plough. After, she'd lock the door carefully, double-check by shaking the door and then shoogle Chemistry gently awake. Up the stairs they'd go to brush their teeth and go to bed. Physics brushed her teeth for a longer time than Chemistry to try to get rid of the smell of smoke.

Sometimes they had two teachers from Lenzie High School round – Rosemary and Nancy, PE and Music, who also, like them, lived together and bought each other comfortable slippers for Christmas. Neither Rosemary and Nancy nor Physics and Chemistry, ever, ever, mentioned the nature of their relationship to each other. Every Boxing Day for the past eight years Rosemary and Nancy came round for dinner. They brought their slippers with them and the four of them sat drinking sweet white sparkling wine with identical moccasins on their feet, enjoying each other's company. Physics, when she had guests round, was always rather proud of Chemistry's adventurous cooking. 'Oh she gets all the proper ingredients, lemon grass, fresh chillies, coriander, glass noodles.'

Rosemary looked flushed and horrified. 'Is that what that taste is – cor-i-an-der?' Rosemary said, exchanging an oh-for-a-turkey-sandwich look with Nancy. 'Which taste?' Chemistry asked, beetroot with pleasure and effort and heat from the cooker.

'That sharpish taste,' said Rosemary, barely hiding her distaste.

'Oh, that'll be lemon grass, definitely,' Chemistry said with authority.

Physics beamed with pride and poured Rosemary and Nancy a little more festive wine. Rosemary covered Nancy's glass with her hand. 'Not for her, she's driving.'

But mostly it was the pair of them alone at the dining table. Sometimes they'd play music after their dinner. Shirley Bassey was a great favourite. One night at the beginning of their relationship, Chemistry had become a little tipsy and had sung along to *Goldfinger*, flourishing her arms in the air and tossing her hair like Shirley Bassey. Then she swung her hips and Physics watched open-mouthed as Chemistry's ample breasts bounced from side to side. It had shocked Physics to the core and excited her. One year Chemistry got them both tickets to go and see Shirley Bassey as a birthday present for Physics.

When they came home that night, Chemistry, bubbling, sang *Hey Big Spender* dancing up and down their living room whilst Physics smoked a rare cigarette indoors. Chemistry leaned right over her when she sang *spend a little time with me* and she sounded, to Physics's ears, exactly like Shirley Bassey. What a woman, what a voice, Physics thought to herself, now as devoted to Bassey as Chemistry was. Physics blew a perfect smoke ring.

That night in bed, Chemistry slid her golden fingers through the fly of Physics pyjamas and touched her gently at first, then firmer, faster; until she felt Physics's whole body stiffen and tremble. Then she lay her hand on Physics's flat stomach and waited until Physics lifted her nightdress with alarming speed, and pushed into her quickly, Physics' long fingers going up and up, deeper and deeper; Chemistry holding on to Physics for dear life. It was so much, first Shirley Bassey, then this, so much she felt she could explode. Outside, the sparkling, experimental stars lit up the suburban sky.

They never discussed these nights. Not a word. Not a single word was spoken or ever had been spoken about such nights. Physics had never ever said the dreaded word out loud for fear of it. The word itself spread terror within her. Chemistry was like her flesh and blood, heart of her heart, a part of her. Chemistry was Physics. Everything was relative. What they did in the dark at night in their own small house in Gleneagles Gardens was immaterial. In the morning Physics could almost feel it disappear like a ghost. But Chemistry knew better. The transformation could be seen on Physics's face, a face that was usually pale and pinched became brighter, more effusive somehow. Her eyes became even more familiar, sparkly. The morning after the night before, Chemistry could not but notice that Physics drove their Mini Metro to school in quite a cavalier fashion, spinning and abruptly whirling the car to a stop in the school car park.

Physics and Chemistry's life altered completely and forever one morning in June when Physics walked into the staff room as usual during the morning break and all the teachers stopped talking. Mr Ferguson coughed awkwardly and Mrs Cameron said loudly, 'The Head wants to see you. I'm afraid a parent has been up.'

'Which parent?' Physics asked.

'Sandra Toner.'

Sandra Toner was Physics's favourite and most talented pupil, a girl she encouraged, gave extra homework to, and had promised to spend thirty minutes extra every Tuesday with her.

'What's the problem?'

Mr Ferguson coughed and said, 'We've no idea.'

Physics looked out of the window in the headmaster's, Mr Smart's office. There was a blur of pupils beyond the glass at break time, one uniform part of another, as if they shared cells. There was the sound of them, high, hysterical, bouncing off the windowpane and back into the playground like a rubber ball. Chemistry was on playground duty; Physics thought she saw her, small and round, in the distance. Mr Smart's face in front of her had changed. There was no doubt about it. It was like witnessing a strange conversion. A man reducing himself. His nose became sharper before Physics's very eyes. He kept moving his tie from side to side as if his collar was much too tight and was about to strangle him any second. His neck lengthening and rising above the collar, appearing for a moment like a snake, high and long, to get some relief, to taste the air. Why don't men like him wear the correct collar size? Physics thought to herself as he informed her he was giving her notice.

'You must understand,' he was saying. 'You must understand it from our point of view as a school. Even if the rumours are unfounded, you understand it is a delicate business, working with young people . . . ' Physics, who rarely said more than a sentence to anybody except Chemistry and her students, kept quite, quite quiet. What was it about?

According to Mr Smart, the school gossiped about the pair of them, saying that they had a lesbian relationship, shared a house, a car, a bed. The whole school. It was time for them to go. He could no longer take the risk. Sandra Toner's father had come to him and said he did not want a lesbian teaching his daughter, especially out of school hours. Physics suddenly came to life. Mr Smart, said, didn't he, the *pair* of them. 'Do you mean to say that you have also sacked Chemistry?' she asked, appalled. 'Who?' Mr Smart asked, puzzled. 'Miss Gibson, you know, Iris. Have you sacked Iris?'

'That's . . . that's what I've been saying,' said Mr Smart, stuttering a bit now. 'Maybe you're too upset to take it all in. I can understand. You've both been exemplary teachers, but I've got the parents to think of.' But Physics wasn't listening any longer. She lunged forward; a voice came out of her as she grabbed hold of his collar and shook him; and shook him again. He was wearing a blue-and-white striped tie. She got hold of the tie and pulled it even tighter. 'You hypocritical bastard! How dare you sack Chemistry,' she shouted at him. 'She is a wonderful teacher. How dare you!' Mr Smart had his arm in the air and was trying to get out of her stranglehold. My God but she was strong for a woman. Suddenly, Physics let go. She gave him one final push and walked out of the headmaster's office, past the school secretary's office, aware that she was being watched, with her head held high, taking long, long strides down the corridor.

Physics and Chemistry's life was never the same since the day they were sacked. Physics now kissed Chemistry in the kitchen over a sizzling wok. Physics stopped wearing skirts altogether. She put all of her checked and pleated and tartan skirts in a big black binbag and drove them to the Cancer Research shop in Springburn. Their new life became experimental, unpredictable. Once they pulled the strings of their curtains closed and lay down on their living room carpet and made love. Sometimes they had been seen at Bishopbriggs Cross, arm in arm at the traffic lights. They opened up a wool shop in Milngavie and called it *Close Knit* – the name made Rosemary and Nancy laugh when they came for their Christmas drink as if they were in on some big secret. It was a strange relief really. Being out of the classroom, the staff room, and the school, selling brightly coloured wool; Shetland wool, Botany wool, mohair, merino, angora, cashmere, cotton, nylon, rayon, wild silk, silk cotton, and patterns, and bobbles and buttons. Plain did the accounts, the opening and closing, the labelling. Purl did the selling, the smiling, the recommending, the ordering. From the very first time, twenty-five years ago, when they had first met, they had this thing between them, this spark. It could always change colour.

In between talking about the elephant

I discover some rough skin on her elbow. I run my tongue along it. I kiss her again then I fetch an apple. A polished red apple. I watch her eat it, even the core. It is thrilling. She holds the apple close to her face and munches slowly and stares at me while she bites into it. The juice from the apple, frothy, slips down the side of her chin. We get out of bed.

We sit down in the middle of the floor in our living room. We are on the twenty-fourth floor. We've got quite a view of our city. Up here, we feel apart, high and holy. I go out as little as possible. I look into her eyes, ready, full of a terrible trembling excitement. I can't wait. It is really all I want to do. It is all she wants to do. My mouth is dry with anticipation. My heart beats faster. I wonder how we lived before, what we did, how we passed our time. It all seems incredible to me that we could have thought life had meaning, significance, depth. How naïve we both were. How shallow. It is not too late. Every day counts.

'The elephant herd,' she says, and I feel a surge of happiness, a pleasure so intense I can feel it in my bones. 'Can you picture them, their brown skin, their long trunks, their vulnerable tusks, their columnar legs, their big feet, with such carefully defined toes, walking in Ceylon before Ceylon was Sri Lanka? Can you just see their big bulging foreheads? Their massive, gifted ears? Imagine the profound feeling they have, elephant to elephant, a clan, a tribe, a family. Oh they know they are similar and different. They know each other's bones!' she shouts out. I feel faint, giddy. I grip the wooden leg of the sofa. 'They're trundling along, together, united in their elephantness, their trunks swaying, their huge hides, swinging. And suddenly one of them falls down and dies. The weight, the crash, makes the earth groan. Maybe it's the matriarch. The other elephants try and get her up: one pushes her with his trunk; another tries putting food in her mouth; another tries to mount her. Some of the elephants stroke and stroke her with their trunks. A calf kneels and tries to suckle. Then the elephant herd circles the dead elephant, round and round. It's a circle of hope, of disbelief. If they just walk round and round this dead elephant, they think they will bring her back to life. Oh, this elephant is not dead, they think; they refuse to believe it. This elephant wouldn't do that to us, they think, one heavy, thunderous step after another. Or perhaps they don't think at all; they carry out actions that are just like our thoughts.

'Still, the dead elephant does not move. They are tired, the top lid of the small eyes heavy and sad and lined. She will not move. What do they do then for her, for our elephant?' She's started to cry. I have tears flooding my face. I wipe them away to the side of my hair with the palm of my hand. She is sniffing into a tissue. I feel protective, aching. We have to get back into bed.

I kiss the tears from her face. If a human being cries from emotion, there is protein in the tears. I lick them. The tears on her cheeks are salty and plump. She moans and sobs and she sounds just like an animal. She moves her head from side to side; her hair is thin, light, feathery.

'When the circus elephant was whipped for not learning its trick,' I tell her after, 'she lay on her side and wept and real tears fell down her elephant's face. The trainer couldn't believe it, the racking sounds of her sobs. He never punished her again. I think some men feel more shame when they mistreat an animal. Isn't it odd how animals can reveal the real man?' I feel pleased with myself.

The light in her eyes has gone out and the dull look has come back. I think she prefers to do the talking. She doesn't like it when I do the talking. I try to make my voice sound soothing, calm, like a balmy hot summer evening in a very foreign place. I try to picture us on some verandah with the sound of foreign birds singing in the heat and trees shuffling gently in the breeze. I imagine us, under the mosquito net, tilting a cold drink down our throats. But my voice can't lift her and take her away.

The phone rings. It will be her mother. ' I won't get it,' I say. 'We're up to our ears here.' Her mother's voice comes on the machine. It grates even though her mother has quite an easy voice. It never used to grate. It has only been an irritant since the elephant. 'Hello it's me. I'm just ringing to see how you are,' she says. Her voice is too cheerful.

The sky is huge outside. A lot is happening in it. Before the elephant we just watched the sky, watched the sun go down in flames and fury and the moon appear cool and serene, we watched the clouds conceal, reveal, conceal the moon. But then the elephant came. And now the sky is just a big sky outside the window. What more is there to say about the sky? When an elephant arrives, you must talk about the elephant. It is impossible to ignore. You must talk about the elephant until you are blue in the face. Because the elephant is massive; because the elephant's brain is larger than yours; because elephants know all about sorrow.

I pull myself away from her to pour a glass of water. The tap runs for a long time and I listen to the sound of the water running. I put the glass to her lips. 'Go on,' I say. 'Go on.' And she does. Oh she does. Her throat is dry at first, so I push the glass of water into her hand and watch while she takes a few careful sips. It's been a long time since we've cooked a proper meal. We've lost interest in food. We eat apples, potatoes and carrots. Mostly we eat them raw, grated. Raw is good, raw is best.

I can't wait for the next instalment. I am glued. If it wasn't for the elephant, I don't know what we would do with our time. 'If it wasn't for the elephant, where would we be?' I sing, but she raises her hand to stop me. Concentrate, she must concentrate. Her face is intent, intense.

'The elephant tribe circles the dead one several times until it comes to an uncertain stop. Then the tribe faces outwards, their trunks hopelessly hanging down to the ground. They tread slowly, slowly, slowly,' (her breathing is uncertain here, difficult) 'circling the dead one. Still they face outwards because they can't face what they see or because that is just their elephant way of doing things. They must know for certain now that all the circles in the world will not bring the dead one back. So they tear off branches from nearby trees, they rip grass clumps from the vegetation and they bring all that back and drop it on the dead one to bury her, to cover her, to show some respect.'

I know what she means. Nothing is lost on me. I listen with huge flapping ears. I could hear her voice if she was miles away and not up in this small living room on the twenty-fourth floor in the city. I hear the voice underneath the voice she speaks with. I hear what it says. If I go out to the shops quickly to get a few essentials, I hear it on my skin. I stand at the till willing the woman to count my change quicker. The money looks strange to me. So do the cars. I rush along the street in the rain with her voice trembling on my skin. She hates me to go out. The lift doors open slowly no matter how many times I press the button. I hurry out of the lift, my key already in my hand.

When I get in, she is awake with the elephant look on her face. I know she has been dying for me to get back. 'Did you know,' she says slowly, 'that when two related groups of elephants meet up again after a long time, there is quite a to-do? Yes!' she says, struggling to sit up, 'They run towards each other screaming and trumpeting. They twine their trunks together like twins. They click their tusks together as if they are saying "Cheers". They spin around each other, rubbing their elephant skin against each other, up and down, up and down. Oh can you see it? Can you just imagine the elephant pleasure of it? All that screaming and rumbling and trumpeting.' I am already at her side, my arms around her. I rest her head on my chest. She is quite out of breath.

We are tired again. We get tired so easily talking about the elephant. Only an elephant can bear an elephant load. We must take it bit by bit. Don't rush. Easy does it. We need to get back into bed. There is nothing else that matters to us.

The sheets are all crumpled so I take them off the bed and I put on fresh white sheets and I lay her down on the bed. Then I go into the bathroom and run the bath and pour some washing powder in it. I throw in the sheets and I take off my shoes and my socks and my jeans. I trample up and down, up and down on the sheets, getting the sweat out, getting the tears out. It is a timeless thing cleaning our sheets like this. We have a washing machine but we don't want to use any of our modern things since the elephant. The sound bothers her. It is a fast whine, a dizzy spin, then the terrible, thunderous rumbling. But I imagine the sound of my feet, walking up and down the bath, slopping and splashing in the soapy water, is soporific. She is falling asleep whilst I clean our sheets.

When I am sure they are clean, I fill the bath again with cold water and I trudge up and down rinsing out the soap with my bare feet. The water is so cold it makes my feet buzz. I pull the plug and let the water run away and I pick up the sheets and wring them, twisting and turning and mangling them with my bare fists till I squeeze out as much water as I possibly can. Squeeze and squeeze and squeeze and squeeze. I carry them through in a basin and hang them on the clothes-horse. 'Imagine I am a mahout,' I say coming into our small, crowded bedroom, with its jungle of clothes hanging everywhere. But she has already dozed off.

So I get into bed beside her and I kiss her shoulder softly.

With my eyes closed, I gently trace her jawbone with my finger. I run my finger round her clavicle, down her breastbone, past her ribs. Every bone is so distinct: hip bone, femur, patella, fibula, tibia, ankle bones. I stop there and work my way back up on the other side this time, going up her back. I know her spine intimately. I open my eyes to find her eyes closed. She likes her bones being traced. Suddenly she sits up and her eyes are bright and elephanty again. We struggle out of bed and I take her arm along the short corridor into the living room where we sit down on the carpet. Whenever we are talking about the elephant, she likes to sit on the carpet.

'This proves it!' she screams. 'There were two African elephant lovers and one died. The other one could not move from the spot where his partner had died. He just stayed and stayed. His herd had to move on without him, through the open grassland, the dry savannah, but he refused to move. It was once thought that elephants went to special places to die, that they had elephant graveyards. In that exact spot in the forest, he stayed. He'd bring things to the spot where she died every day, gifts – branches, leaves, long grasses, a special piece of bark. Years passed and his elephant partner disintegrated bit by bit till all that was left were her bones. He picked up her tusk, his favourite bone of hers, running his trunk over the bone and smelling it, turning it over and then he went off with it. Elephants have always had a strong interest in bones. He walked and walked for several days and several nights until he found his herd. He was carrying her tusk in his mouth. They all gathered round and stroked the tusk with their trunks. They knew who it was, don't you see! A baby calf once found her mother's jawbone and lay stroking it for hours because she recognized her mother's face. You would recognize mine wouldn't you, darling?' she says, sighing pleasantly. 'If you just found my jawbone, you would know it was me, wouldn't you, sweetheart?' 'Of course I would,' I tell her. I put a cushion under her head for her to doze a little. Perhaps she might dream a dream about the Indian elephant, the *Elephas maximus*.

Our house is so quiet. There is the sound of my lover breathing, that's all. I go into the kitchen to make some broth, some potato broth. Everything has to be very simple. No oil. I chop the shallots small and put them in our soup pot adding a small amount of water. No Garlic – much too strong. No salt, no pepper, no caraway seeds. I can't risk any flavour at all. I peel the potatoes. Skins are too difficult now. I bring it to boil then simmer. Last week I made a stew. But we are beyond stews now. Simmer, soup, bed, elephant. My life is right down to the bare essentials now. I clean up after myself. The elephant has changed me into a very tidy person. These days mess makes me weep. I have to have clean bare surfaces. She has to have clean sheets. I long to rip all our clothes off our hangers, to strip our wardrobe till we have very little left. If I could stare into our dark wardrobe and see empty space, I would feel uplifted.

So I pull back the crisp, clean sheets and tuck her in. She is exhausted and her limbs are thinner than the day before and the day before that. 'The Indian elephant is sometimes said to weep,' I whisper in her ear, before she drifts off to sleep. 'Darwin said that.'

A little later, she manages some of my broth. Perhaps four whole teaspoons full. She seems to gain some strength from my broth, some sustenance. It is astonishing when she comes back round like this, her eyes alert and her voice strong. 'You know, Ganesh,' she says. 'You know the Hindus have an elephant God.' She drifts off again and doesn't say anymore for two days.

I feed her the juice of an orange one day. When she sleeps, I polish my shoes till they shine deep and dark. If I have to go out, I hurry down and grab what we need from the corner shop, then I rush back up. It seems bizarre to me that people are still going about their business. The minute I come into our flat I can smell her smell. My nose is so strong now. I wipe it with my arm. There is nothing for me to do. Our kitchen is bare and clean. I fill the kettle and make two cups of tea. I put sugar in both cups even though neither of us has sugar. I know the night ahead will be long and dark and will seem as if it could go on forever. At some point, the point I will be waiting for, the night will turn round and be heading at last for morning. Like a ship coming into the shore.

We fall in and out of sleep and in and out of each other's dreams, tossing and turning and sometimes she cries out. In the middle of the night she sits bolt upright and wants to make it down to the carpet again. I carry her into our living room, beside myself with tiredness, not knowing if I am up to the elephant in the middle of the night. I bring a sheet and cover her.

She needs water, but she can't manage it on her own. I get a straw from the kitchen and she attempts to suck it up, but even that is too much for her. I fill a flannel with cold water and squeeze it into her mouth. Her tongue comes right out and licks the drops. I put my fingers in a glass of water and then put them in her mouth. I rub her tongue with my wet fingers. I know her tongue too. I know all of her. 'There was an elephant, who got separated from her herd and couldn't find a waterhole,' I begin, but she grabs me and whispers urgently, hoarsely 'Tell me about the ears!'

'You know what they say about elephant ears? They can hear low sounds from miles away, they pick up the sonic booms? A deep rumbling, a vibrating sound. The elephant can hear the sound through its own trembling skin.' She nods, her eyes closed, but I can tell she is listening. Her cheeks are open and wide, almost new. I lightly touch her face. She opens her eyes for a second, takes me in and then closes them again. I take her hand in mine and she holds it for a moment. Then she starts to pluck at the sheet with her hands, pluck, pluck, pluck.

'It comes after the trumpet signal has been given. A herd of elephants lived in a free park in Zimbabwe many miles away from another herd of elephants who were about to be culled. On the day of the culling the free elephants, miles and miles away, rushed to the very back of their park. They wept and the sound of those elephants weeping was electrifying.'

I imagine them. They fill my whole head. She falls off to sleep again and I pick her up and carry her to our bed. She is light now, skin and bone and there is nothing I can do. There is nothing I can do. Only the elephant can help, only the kind, compassionate, understanding elephant can help us now. I love to see the excitement in her eyes, the tenderness, the elephant empathy. It is quite exhilarating. We could never have said the things we say to each other, were it not for the enormous elephant.

Perhaps she sleeps for an hour, at the most two. But suddenly she wakes up, screaming. She is having the nightmare. I rush and get her medication and give it to her with some water. I'm here, I tell her. Don't worry. Try and sleep. But she is too restless. I carry her into the living room again and try to make her comfortable.

'Did you know about the baby African elephants

that witnessed their families' slaughter by poachers, witnessed the tusks being cut off their bodies? These baby African elephants woke themselves up in the night for months afterwards, screaming. Elephants scream, don't they? The scream comes out of their long trunk and goes right up into the air.' I am keeping my promise to her. Don't stop talking about the elephant till it happens, she said when we heard. She smiles at me, the weakest of smiles. Her eyes take me in and then she loses it. I want her to stay awake. 'Did you know elephants can draw pictures?' I ask, certain that this will make her open her eyes. 'They draw pictures on the ground with sticks.' But she has drifted off; she won't come back.

I go to the kitchen to make her some hot potato broth. It is the middle of the night and I am here making soup. I open the curtains in our kitchen and look down. I can see the lights from cars move slowly along the roads, the lights from other buildings sparkle and spray. They look alive, the lights, dancing and twirling, pretty. The road is a long black scarf and the lights are jewels. I used to love being driven in a car at night, half asleep, watching the bright lights outside. It used to make me feel safe. I stare down for ages. I see a tiny man in a dark coat hurrying along the street. I can even see that he is smoking from here. A tiny light is in his hand. Everything is really very small.

I know that if I can just get her to take a few spoonfuls of soup, she will be the better for it. I try and sit her up and spoon-feed her my broth but her mouth won't accept it. Her eyes won't open. Her body is heavy. She can't be hungry. I put a pillow under her head and sing to her. I stroke her long bones, her damp hair. It is sparse now, her hair, thin on the ground. She is not her usual colour. She is grey. I walk round and round her facing out towards our window. I walk around our small flat, going from room to room. From our bedroom to the bathroom, from the bathroom to the living room, from the living room to the kitchen. I find a shell and a stone in the bathroom. I carry them into the living room. I find an old photograph of her mother. I lie it beside her. I search for her favourite scarf ripping things out of her drawers till I find it. I hold it to myself first. It is full of her smell. The sun is frail and rising in the sky. The light outside is pale and weak. I look down again out of our window. Down there, the whole world looks different in the day. There are many bright cars on the motorway. I can't see speed from up here. They seem to float. I look across at all the buildings, the shops and the offices and the houses and the homes. I look down at the trees. It all looks pretend. When birds fly past the window, I can't believe they are real.

I sprinkle her with spring water. I go back to our room and carry all of our pillows through and lay them around her. I try kissing her, touching her. But she doesn't respond. Her body is warm but she will not move. I rest my head on her chest and hold her cheek. For a split second I am sure I can feel her breath on my face. Then I realize it is my own breath coming back to me. So I get up. I trudge round and round her again. I keep on going, around and around and around. I face away from her. The light outside darkens. It seems to darken inch by inch by inch. I know what to do. We have talked about this. I bring sheets from our bed and cover her and then I lie down beside her and I hold her. I won't leave her. I will stay with her. I won't leave her. Outside the big bulk of darkness presses against our window. There's a slither of moon in the sky like a tusk.

JACKIE KAY

Trumpet

PICADOR

Ostensibly recounting the life and death of Joss Moody, famous jazz musician, *Trumpet* also explores themes of love, loyalty and family. Beginning in the days immediately following Joss's funeral, the story is told through various different voices, each offering their own tantalizing glimpses into the world of this enigmatic central character: trumpeter, husband, foster-father, subject of a tell-all biography – and once a woman called Josephine. Kay's writing is sympathetic yet unsentimental, and she draws the reader into Joss's story even while he waits in the wings, never quite known, except through the words of others.

'In this extraordinary first novel, Kay has combined a love story with a mystery, thriller and case of deliberate mistaken identity to devastating effect'

Big Issue

'The book's style works like a jazz riff, a literary improvisation of the central melody of Joss's death'

Independent on Sunday

EMILY PERKINS

The New Girl

PICADOR

It is the beginning of the summer holiday in a town in the middle of nowhere. Julia and her best friends Chicky and Rachel are school leavers emerging from their girlhood, waiting for the future. While they wait, Miranda, an exotically beautiful woman from the city, arrives to teach a summer class. And after her arrival, nothing will ever be the same again.

'A quietly powerful tale of growing up'
Guardian

'Perkins has created an unforgettable narrative of female teenage coming of age: its poetic tenderness and acute honesty will give painful stabs of recognition'
Evening Standard

CAROL ANN DUFFY

The World's Wife

PICADOR

'She reveals the foibles of the great, the ghastly and the ordinary bloke and the sufferings of those closest to them. The result is a melange of history lesson, fairy tale and modern-day domestic tragedy, with the occasional joke thrown in for good measure . . . Duffy's poetics are flawless – she never misses a beat, her pace is exhilarating, and her language is original and exciting'
Scotsman

'Duffy takes a cheeky, subversive, no-nonsense swipe with a dish of clout at the famous men of history and myth. They don't have a chance in hell of dodging her quick-witted wallop as she relays their stories from their spouse's point of view . . . Reading Duffy's dramatic monologues is a bit like overhearing a conversation in a ladies' lavatory. You can almost imagine Mrs Midas touching up her make-up in the mirror as she moans about her husband'
The Times